SECRETS

It wasn't fair, Jessica raged, tears streaming down her face. Enid was going to the fall dance with Ronnie, and she was sure to be named queen. Ronnie was so blind with love that he'd swing a million votes her way.

Jessica sighed. She just *had* to win. If she were queen, Bruce Patman would finally notice her. She'd never wanted anything so badly in her entire life. She'd do anything to make it happen.

Out of the corner of one wet eye, Jessica glimpsed a piece of paper sticking out from under the bed. It looked like a letter.

"Dear Enid," she read with a sudden voracious interest. A smile crept slowly across her features as a plan shaped itself in her mind.

Bantam Books in the Sweet Valley High Series
Ask your bookseller for the books you have missed

SWEET VALLEY HIGH

SECRETS

Written by
Kate William

Created by
FRANCINE PASCAL

BANTAM BOOKS
TORONTO • NEW YORK • LONDON • SYDNEY • AUCKLAND

RL 6, IL age 12 and up

SECRETS
A Bantam Book / November 1983
11 printings through April 1986

Sweet Valley High is a trademark of Francine Pascal

Conceived by Francine Pascal

Produced by Cloverdale Press Inc.

Cover art by James Mathewuse

ISBN 0-553-25044-2

Published simultaneously in the United States and Canada

Bantam Books are published by Bantam Books, Inc. Its trademark, consisting of the words "Bantam Books" and the portrayal of a rooster, is Registered in U.S. Patent and Trademark Office and in other countries. Marca Registrada. Bantam Books, Inc., 666 Fifth Avenue, New York, New York 10103.

PRINTED IN THE UNITED STATES OF AMERICA

O   20 19 18 17

SECRETS

One

"My very own sister! How could she do such a hideous thing to me?" Jessica Wakefield fumed.

She shimmied into the dress she was wearing for her date with Tom McKay. Her best friend, Cara Walker, zipped her up, then stepped back and sighed. Jessica was, as usual, too gorgeous for words. Her sun-colored hair shimmered about tanned shoulders left bare by the silky Hawaiian print sun dress that perfectly complemented her blue-green eyes. A bewitching smile on her lovely oval face usually completed the picture of perfection. The only trouble was, she wasn't smiling right now.

"Look at me," Jessica ranted. "I'm an absolute mess! I haven't been able to do a single thing with my hair since this afternoon." She tossed

1

her head in disgust, even though every golden strand seemed to be in place. "Can you imagine— being dunked with every stitch on? How positively humiliating!"

She shuddered at the memory. She'd been tricked—and by her very own twin sister, Elizabeth, who practically always shielded Jessica above and beyond the call of sisterly duty. It was almost too much to be believed. Jessica had been tossed, fully clothed, into the Sweet Valley High pool, the students' annual playful punishment for the author of the "Eyes and Ears" gossip column of the school paper. However, it was Elizabeth who was the columnist, but she'd engineered a mix-up in identity, a trick she'd picked up, no doubt, from Jessica herself.

Cara giggled. "I don't know. I thought you looked kind of cute. Even though you probably deserved to look like a drowned rat. You know, you really *did* have it coming after what you told me you pulled on Liz."

Jessica cut her dead with a glare. "You're lucky we're at your house instead of mine, or I'd really let you have it." Deep down, though, she knew she'd deserved it, too.

"Oh, come on, Jess, you know you really did look kind of sexy. Like Bo Derek in that beach scene in *10*."

A smile pulled at the corners of Jessica's mouth, and the harder she tried to keep a straight face, the worse it got. Finally she collapsed, laughing, onto Cara's bed.

"I did, didn't I? Even so, it *was* humiliating being set up like that." A thought occurred to her, and she clapped a hand over her mouth, sobering instantly. "Oh, Cara, I hope Bruce didn't see me. I'd die!"

She'd been in love with Bruce Patman since her freshman year. He was the most desirable guy in school. Besides being movie-star handsome, he was fabulously rich and drove a terrific black Porsche.

"Just keep thinking of how you'll feel when you're queen of the fall dance," Cara cajoled as she stood in front of the mirror, combing out her own shiny dark hair. "Bruce will be so blinded by your beauty he won't remember anything else."

Jessica wondered if even Cara knew just how badly she wanted that crown. The dance was two weeks away, and she could hardly wait. Bruce had been nominated for king, and it seemed a cinch he would win. None of the other nominees even came close. If she won, too, it would mean reigning at Bruce's side for many of the school-related activities during the semester. It would mean that, finally, Bruce would have to notice her—and, naturally, fall in love with her.

Winning that crown meant everything to her. And when Jessica Wakefield set out to get something, she let nothing and no one stand in her way. Usually it wasn't hard to get what she wanted. With her bewitching looks and beguiling ways, few people ever realized they'd been had by Jessica until it was too late.

Elizabeth Wakefield stared down at the shattered remains of the measuring cup her best friend, Enid Rollins, had just dropped.

"Oh, Liz, I'm sorry!" Enid cried, her eyes filling with tears. "I don't know what happened. It—it just slipped out of my hands!"

Elizabeth hugged her best friend, forgetting the fact that they were both covered in chocolate-chip cookie batter. Enid Rollins was spending the night at the Wakefields', and Elizabeth had initiated Project C.C. Cookie in the hope it would distract Enid from whatever it was she'd been so jumpy about all evening. Actually, Elizabeth had been noticing a nervous edge to Enid's behavior ever since she'd started going with Ronnie Edwards about two months earlier, but she hadn't wanted to pry. She figured Enid would tell her what was bothering her when she was ready. She didn't believe that being best friends with someone entitled her to pry into her friend's private business. But Enid had been in tears when she arrived, too upset even to talk, and things had gone downhill from there. This had gone too far.

"Forget the stupid cup," Elizabeth said. "What's *wrong*, Enid? You don't have to tell me if you don't want to, but just remember I'm your friend. I'm here to help if you need it."

Enid covered her face with her hands. Elizabeth noticed that they were trembling. "Oh, Liz, I'm so afraid!"

"Of *what?*"

"Of losing Ronnie. If he knew the truth about me, he'd hate me. Absolutely *despise* me!"

"How could he possibly hate you?" Elizabeth asked. "The only truth is that you're a fantastic person."

Enid shook her head. "You don't know, Liz. I've even been afraid to tell you. I didn't want you to hate me, either."

"I could never hate you, Enid."

"Maybe not, but I just know Ronnie would if he found out."

"OK, what's this terrible secret?" Elizabeth smiled in an attempt to lighten Enid's misery. "You're really a cat burglar, right? Straight-A student by day, jewel thief by night."

"Come on, Liz, it's not funny." Enid refused to be consoled. A tear trickled down one chocolate-smudged cheek.

"I'm sorry," Elizabeth said. "Really I am. It's just that I can't believe anything you did could be as terrible as all that."

Enid took a deep, shaky breath, then blurted, "Try a police record, then."

"You?" In spite of herself, Elizabeth couldn't help being shocked.

"Yeah, me. Oh, I know what you're thinking. Straight-as-an-arrow Enid. But I wasn't always so straight."

Enid haltingly poured out to her best friend the story that had burdened her for so long. Two years earlier, when her parents were getting divorced, she'd gone a little crazy. She was angry, hurt, upset. She'd drifted in with a bad crowd and gotten involved with a boy named George Warren. They'd gone from drinking to drugs—trying just about everything that came their way.

The situation came to a nightmarish climax the afternoon Enid and George went joyriding in George's GTO—stoned out of their minds—and struck a little boy who was playing near the road. For Enid the whole world stopped moving at that moment. She climbed out of the car as if in slow motion, her knees rubbery. Forever frozen in her memory was the sight of that tiny figure crumpled on the pavement, the horrifying sound of the scream of his mother as she came racing out of her house. Enid stood there as if paralyzed. A voice that didn't seem to be coming from her kept saying, over and over, "I'm sorry. I'm so sorry."

Luckily, the boy wasn't seriously injured. He'd suffered a broken arm and a mild concussion. Enid and George were arrested, but placed on six months' probation and signed into a drug counseling program at Juvenile Hall. Enid emerged from the experience a different person. She'd been shocked into seeing the roller-coaster ride of self-destruction she'd been on, and she'd set about putting her feet on solid ground. She was straight now, with grades to match. She hadn't seen George in two years, since his parents had sent him away to a strict private boarding school.

The whole time she'd been telling her story, Enid was staring down at the kitchen counter, unable to meet Elizabeth's gaze. Now she looked up into a pair of blue-green eyes shining with sympathy. Enid had always thought Elizabeth was pretty—though in a less flashy way than her identical twin sister Jessica—but it was a sparkle that went beyond her all-American good looks, the perfect white teeth, the spun-sunshine hair. Elizabeth was a person who *cared*. She was the first person in whom Enid had been able to confide her terrible secret. Somehow, deep down, she must have known that Elizabeth wouldn't condemn her.

"I'm glad you told me," Elizabeth said. "But it doesn't change a thing. You're still my best friend, and I *still* think you're a fantastic person. Even more fantastic than ever, now that I know what you've been through."

Enid was crying openly now, the tears pouring down her face. Part of it was the sheer relief of being able to unburden herself at last, but mostly she was still in agony over the fear of what would happen if the one person she *didn't* want to know should find out.

She forced a quavery smile. "Tell that to Ronnie. I'll bet he wouldn't think I was so terrific if he knew I'd been lying to him all this time."

"You haven't exactly lied to him," Elizabeth pointed out.

"I haven't exactly told the truth, either."

"Come on, Enid, it's not the most hideous secret in the world, no matter how bad it must have seemed at the time. Besides, it was two years ago—that's practically prehistoric by now."

"Easy for you to say. You don't have any skeletons in your closet."

"If I did, Jessica would've borrowed them." Elizabeth couldn't suppress a tiny smile, thinking of her twin's charming little habit of foraging in her closet whenever she ran out of her own things to wear.

"You wouldn't think it was so funny if you were in danger of losing Todd," Enid insisted.

"I know if it were me, I'd tell Todd. If Ronnie really loves you, he'll understand."

"Oh, Liz, you just don't know!"

Sighing, Enid sank down in the kitchen chair by the window that overlooked the patio. She stared mournfully out over the glassy surface of the lighted pool, shimmering sapphire against the backdrop of darkness. The exact blue of Ronnie's eyes, Enid noted.

"Ronnie's not like Todd," Enid explained. "He expects one hundred percent of my attention. If he knew about George . . ." She stopped, biting her lip.

"What about George? You said yourself you haven't seen him in a couple of years."

"It's true I haven't actually *seen* him. But"— she released a deep sigh—"we write to each other. It's not what you think. I mean, there's nothing going on between us. We're just friends. I started writing to George because he was so mixed-up and unhappy. I wanted him to know it didn't have to be that way forever."

"I think it's nice that you're helping George," Elizabeth said. "There's no reason Ronnie should be jealous over a few friendly letters."

Enid groaned. "You're talking about someone who turns green if I look sideways at another guy by accident. Last week he caught me going over a homework assignment with a guy in my history class. I thought he was going to blow a fuse!"

A tiny alarm went off inside Elizabeth. "But if you explained it just the way you did to me . . ."

"He still wouldn't understand." Enid slumped forward against the table, burying her face in her arms. "I just know I'm going to lose him!"

Elizabeth laid a comforting hand on Enid's

9

shoulder. "Look at it this way. Nobody knows about these letters except you and me, right?"

"Right."

"So what's got you suddenly so afraid Ronnie will find out?"

"It's George," Enid explained. "In his last letter he said he's coming back to Sweet Valley for a visit in less than two weeks. He's come back before, but this time he wants to see me."

Up in Elizabeth's room Enid dug a sheaf of letters out of her overnight bag. "I brought them along, hoping I'd have the nerve to tell you," she said sheepishly, handing them over to Elizabeth.

Elizabeth read the one on top—George's most recent letter:

Dear Enid,

As you know, I've been keeping pretty busy with exams. They really sock it to us here, which I didn't like at first, but now I'm glad they do. I guess I've been pretty much of a goof-off all my life, so I've had a lot of catching up to do. Studying isn't exactly my idea of having a good time, but in a funny way it really kind of grows on you. I feel better about everything in general, as you know from my other letters. I used to be angry all the time, blaming my parents and everyone else for what was wrong with my life, but I think who I was really mad at was me. I don't want to sound weird or anything, but you helped me see that more than anyone, Enid. You'll never know how much your letters meant to me. I don't mind admitting to you that it was pretty depressing here at first. This is definitely *not* Disneyland. But I won't be here much longer—only until the end of the semester when I'll finally have enough credits to graduate—and the future is looking pretty good. I'm glad to hear things are going so well for you, too. Your last letter was definitely an upper (the only kind I go for these days). I'd really like to see you when I come home this time, but I'll understand if you'd rather not.

Love,
George

P.S. Thanks again for the brownies you sent on my birthday. They disappeared in about two seconds, but they were good while they lasted.
P.P.S. Say hi to my buddy Winston for me.

"I don't know what to do," Enid said when Elizabeth had put the letter down. "I don't want to stop being George's friend, but I *can't* see him. Ronnie would take it all wrong."

"I should think Ronnie would be glad to know how loyal you are to people you care about."

Enid shook her head with stubborn insistence. "It would be the ultimate end. He'd be furious. I'd lose him." She clutched at Elizabeth's arm. "Liz, you've got to promise me you won't tell anyone about the letters. Swear you won't!"

"Cross my heart, hope to die."

Solemnly Elizabeth placed her palm against the nearest thick book at hand, which just happened to be her dictionary. Being a writer, she was never very far from it. Of course, she didn't consider herself an Ernest Hemingway. Not yet, anyway. Right now most of the writing she did was for Sweet Valley High's *Oracle,* for which she was author of the "Eyes and Ears" column.

Elizabeth understood Enid's fear of having something like this leak out. Sweet Valley was still a small town, despite its rapidly growing silicon chip industry. And in small towns, as her father said, rumors had a tendency to multiply like mice in a cornfield.

In many ways Sweet Valley High was the biggest mousetrap of all—the cafeteria, the locker rooms, and the front lawn were favorite centers of communication on every subject from the color of someone's hair to scandals involving drugs and who was fooling around with whom. Most of the gossip was harmless, but occasionally a vicious rumor would spread like wildfire, burning innocent people in the process. Elizabeth recently had been on the receiving end of such a rumor herself, when her eternally two-faced twin was nearly arrested and let the police think she was Elizabeth. The cruel gossip had disturbed Elizabeth greatly, so she was in a better position than most to appreciate Enid's dilemma.

"I swear that if I ever tell about the letters, you can, uh—" Elizabeth grinned as inspiration struck. "You can bury me alive in chocolate-chip cookie batter!"

Enid moaned, holding her stomach. Both girls had eaten so many cookies they were sure they were going to gain at least fifty pounds apiece. But the joke had the desired effect of getting Enid to smile.

"Ugh!" Enid said. "I think I'll just take your word for it. I trust you, Liz, I really do. You're my very best friend."

"I should hope so." Elizabeth laughed, pretending to smother Enid with her pillow. "Who else would invite you to spend the night with the way you snore?"

"I don't snore!" Enid protested, leaping off the bed and dissolving into giggles as she beaned Elizabeth with her own pillow.

"Like a seven forty-seven at takeoff!" came Elizabeth's muffled shriek.

In all the commotion, neither girl noticed as one of George's letters fell to the carpet.

"I give—I give!" Elizabeth gasped at last.

13

"Come on, let's get into bed. We can tell ghost stories. I know a good one about these two teenage girls left all alone in this big creepy house. . . ."

"Elizabeth Wakefield!" Enid cried. "If you tell me one of your ghost stories, I'll never get any sleep. The last time I couldn't sleep for a week."

Elizabeth smelled a challenge—and rose to it. She flicked off the bedside lamp, plunging the room into shadowy darkness.

"It was a dark and stormy night. . . ." she intoned in her creakiest voice.

Enid settled back with a sigh of defeat, secretly glad to get her mind off the real-life fear that was pressing down on her. The thought of losing Ronnie was the worst nightmare she could imagine.

Two

Jessica stared restlessly out the window at the sloping green lawns of Sweet Valley High as Ms. Nora Dalton droned on and on, something to do with conjugating French verbs.

Bore, bored, boring, Jessica conjugated in her mind. It was such a gorgeous day, she wished she were at the beach instead, soaking up the rays in the bronze, wet-look, one-piece she'd bought the week before at Foxy Mama.

Out of the corner of her eye she caught Winston Egbert, seated across the aisle, gazing at her with a goofy, lovesick expression. Yech! Did he have to stare at her like that? Even so, she found herself shifting slightly to a more flattering pose.

"We're ready whenever you are, Jessica."

Jessica whipped about to find herself under the sudden scrutiny of Ms. Dalton, a tall, slender woman in her twenties, whose wide-set hazel eyes regarded her with a hint of knowing amusement.

"Sorry," Jessica said, "I didn't get the question."

"I was just wondering if you might like to let us in on the secret," Ms. Dalton said, her smile widening. She didn't smile often, but when she did, her normally pretty but serious face lit up to spectacular effect.

"Secret?" Jessica echoed, growing distinctly uncomfortable.

"*Oui.* The secret of how you expect to conjugate the verbs I've written on the board if you're not looking at it," she needled in a pleasant voice.

"Mental telepathy!" Winston piped, swooping to her rescue with clownish gallantry. "She's really Wonder Woman in disguise. Hey, Jess, show us how you leap tall buildings in a single bound."

"That's Superman, dummy," Ken Matthews said from the back of the classroom, where he sat with his long legs sprawled across the aisle. Ken also had a tendency to shoot off his mouth whenever the occasion arose. The difference between Ken and Winston was that Ken was tall, blond, gorgeous, and captain of the football team. "And you'll be out of here faster than a speeding bullet if you don't put a lid on it."

"Thank you, Ken," their teacher put in dryly.

16

"I think we can *all* settle down and get some work done now. Unless," she added, eyes sparkling, "any of you has X-ray vision and can see the answers I have hidden in my desk."

A ripple of laughter greeted this. Ken flashed her one of his thousand-watt grins. It was common knowledge that Ken was hopelessly in love with Ms. Dalton, who had been giving him extra tutoring after class to boost his near-failing grade. Even so, Jessica doubted that Ms. Dalton suspected that Ken had a crush on her.

Teachers could be so *dense* about some things, she thought. *She* was always the first to know it when a guy liked her—as well as the first to take advantage of it when it suited her. Even Winston might come in handy one of these days. The trouble was that right now the only one she really wanted was Bruce Patman, and she might as well live on the moon as far as he was concerned.

Jessica conjured up an image of Bruce—fabulously rich, popular, superstar-handsome Bruce of the ice-blue eyes and coal-black Porsche. If only he would ask her to the fall dance. . . .

Of course, there *was* a way, even if he didn't ask her. Jessica had been nominated for queen. Bruce Patman was up for king. She played out the scenario in her mind. There she would be, utterly ravishing, pretending to look shocked that her name had been chosen. She would glide demurely up to the stage, the merest hint of a tear trembling on her lower lashes—not enough to smudge her eyeliner—as she bowed her head in humble acceptance of the crown.

Naturally, Bruce would be chosen king. He was easily the best-looking boy in school. He would smile at her and take her hand, and the two of them would drift onto the dance floor for a solo dance under the spotlight, as if they were the only two people in the world.

She simply *had* to win. It was her big chance to make Bruce fall in love with her. The dance was only two weeks away, and Jessica was desperate to find a way of winning the crown for sure. She would do anything, absolutely *anything*, to be queen. . . .

She was jolted from her daydream by the harsh jingle of the bell and the mad dash for the door.

Lila Fowler detached herself from the mob, falling in step with Jessica as she made her way toward the lockers, still caught up in the pink haze of her daydream.

"Don't you just *hate* her?" Lila hissed, a scowl twisting her pretty features.

"Who?" Jessica asked.

"Dalton. Who else? Didn't you care that she made a fool of you in front of the entire class?"

"Bite your tongue," Jessica returned blithely. "Nobody makes a fool of me. Least of all a cream puff like Ms. Dalton. Actually, she's not so bad. I kind of like her, even if she *is* a teacher."

Ms. Dalton was one of the newer teachers at Sweet Valley High, so naturally there was a good deal of speculation about her. A lot of it had to do with her being young and pretty—a fact that wasn't lost on the male population of SVH, especially Mr. Roger Collins, faculty adviser for the school paper and resident "hunk" among the male teachers.

Jessica had learned that Ms. Dalton had recently begun dating Lila's divorced father, George Fowler. Anything to do with the Fowlers, one of the richest families in Sweet Valley, was news.

Lila enjoyed the attention, but what she didn't enjoy was the awful *thing* that was going on between her father and Nora Dalton. Jessica suspected that Lila was jealous. She was always vying for his attention, though it seemed as if he never had had enough time for her. Now that Ms. Dalton had entered the picture, he would have even less.

"I don't blame Daddy so much, even if he *is* being incredibly naive," Lila was saying. "After all, she practically threw herself at him. I'm positive she's only after his money."

Jessica wasn't normally in the habit of defending people, but even she thought Lila had gone overboard on the subject.

"Come on, Lila," she cajoled. "I just don't think Ms. Dalton is the man-eater type."

Lila shot her a look of disdain. "They're the worst kind, don't you see? The ones who don't *seem* the type. I mean, look at the way she keeps Ken Matthews dangling, for instance. It's positively disgusting!"

"Ken?" Jessica snorted. "I think you're just jealous because he'll be thinking of Ms. Dalton while he's at the dance with you."

"I am *not* jealous. Just because Ken's taking me to the dance doesn't make him the love of my life. Why should I care if he's got the hots for some other girl?"

"Girl? Lila, honey, Ms. Dalton is practically old enough to be his mother, for heaven's sake!"

"She's twenty-five," Lila replied haughtily. "I asked my father. That makes her exactly nine years older than us."

"It still doesn't explain why she'd be interested in Kenny. I mean, I know he'd probably jump off the Golden Gate Bridge if she asked him to, but—"

"Don't you see?" Lila broke in. She yanked her locker open savagely. "She's too subtle for anything *that* obvious. I'll bet there's a whole lot that we don't know about. I've seen the way she drapes herself across his desk when they're alone in the classroom."

"Really? I hadn't noticed." Jessica peered into the small mirror that was taped to the inside of the locker door as she concentrated on applying a fresh coat of Plum Passion gloss to her lips.

Actually, if Ms. Dalton was having an affair with Ken Matthews, it might even liven things up at school, she thought.

"I wish I could catch her *really* doing something with Ken," Lila muttered. "Then my father'd see what she's like under all that nicey-nice."

"Catch who?" Cara Walker strolled up beside them, her eyes alight with curiosity.

Cara was always looking for fresh gossip. It was one of the reasons she and Jessica were such good friends. Cara was content to let Hurricane Jessica make all the waves, while she followed in her wake, gathering up the debris of gossip that littered her path. With her sleek, dark good looks, Cara was pretty and popular in her own right, though certainly no match for the stunning Jessica—a crucial point in her favor, as far as Jessica was concerned.

"Ms. Dalton," Jessica drawled, forming her mouth into a sexy pout as she looked at herself in the mirror. "Lila's convinced she and Ken Matthews are having some kind of passionate affair."

"*What?*" Cara screeched. This was almost too good to be true. "I don't believe it!"

"Believe it," snapped Lila, slamming her locker shut with an ear-splitting clang.

"You mean, you've actually seen them—"

The rest of Cara's question was swallowed up as the second bell shattered the air. Jessica and

Cara both slammed their lockers shut, then locked them.

"Got to rush," said Lila. "I don't want to be late for choir. They're choosing soloists today for the Christmas program. "I'll just die if I don't get lead soprano!"

"Don't worry," Cara assured her. "I overheard Ms. Bellesario in the office telling old Chrome Dome that you were a sure thing."

Lila's brooding expression switched to a look of stunned happiness. First she hugged Cara, then Jessica, who squealed aloud in protest.

"Hey, watch it! You're going to smudge my masterpiece. I want to look absolutely perfect in case I happen to run into you-know-who."

Cara cast Jessica a knowing grin as she waved goodbye to Lila. "You-know-who's initials wouldn't happen to be B.P., by any chance, would they?"

"You've got it." Jessica giggled. "For Beautiful Person."

"Or maybe Black Porsche," Cara joked.

"You have to admit," said Jessica, "there *is* something wildly sexy about a man in a black Porsche—especially if he's six feet plus and has gorgeous blue eyes and is incredibly rich," she added.

Jessica sighed. She'd never wanted anything so badly in her entire life as she wanted to go to the dance with Bruce. It was a new feeling for her. She was used to getting what she wanted—

one way or another. And yet half the time Bruce acted as if he scarcely noticed she was alive, even though she'd done everything she could to get him to notice. Like the time she'd dropped half a ton of books right at his feet in study hall. Bruce had only grinned lazily and without lifting a single finger to help her pick anything up, commented, "Way to go, Wakefield."

This time she wasn't going to let him slide out of her grasp so easily. She had an idea. "Hey, Cara," she said, linking arms with her best friend as they strolled off toward class. "You sit next to Ronnie Edwards in history, don't you?"

"What of it? Got your eye on him, too? I don't blame you. He's not bad-looking."

"He's also head of the dance committee," Jessica put in quickly. "I was just wondering if you would feel him out for me. You know, next time you're talking to him, sort of casually try to influence him to get kids to vote for me."

"Sure thing," said Cara. "But frankly, Jess, I don't see what you're so worried about. I mean, look at the competition, will you? Enid Rollins, for instance. You're about a million times prettier."

Jessica's eyes narrowed at the mention of Enid's name. "Yeah, Enid's a nerd, all right, but she happens to be Ronnie's girlfriend, remember? He could get a lot of people to vote for her."

Cara shrugged. "Who knows? Maybe they'll break up before then."

"No way. Have you seen how they act around each other? You'd think they were joined at the hip!"

"Make that joined at the lip." Cara giggled.

But Jessica was too busy boiling to take notice. She had other reasons for disliking Enid, mainly the fact that lately she seemed to be taking up every spare minute of Elizabeth's time. Time Elizabeth could be spending with her adorable, fun-loving twin sister instead.

"Frankly," Jessica said, "I can't imagine what a cute guy like Ronnie sees in that little creep."

"Liz seems to like her pretty well, too," commented Cara, casting Jessica a sidelong glance.

"Liz!" Jessica snorted in disgust. "Listen, Cara, my sister has absolutely *no* taste when it comes to picking friends. It's positively embarrassing! I mean, what if someone thought it was *me* hanging out with Enid?"

As they turned the corner, Jessica caught sight of Bruce Patman in the crowded corridor. He was loping toward the staircase, looking impossibly gorgeous, as usual, in a pair of off-white cords and a heather-blue sweater that matched his eyes. Her knees went weak as warm Jell-O, and her heart thundered in her ears.

"I've got to go. I'll talk to you later," she tossed distractedly back at Cara, her eyes riveted on the glorious spectacle of Bruce climbing the stairs with the loose-limbed grace of a young lion.

Perfection, Jessica thought, feeling herself grow warm and prickly all over. Bruce was absolute perfection, from his toes to his carelessly tousled dark hair. He looked airbrushed, as if he'd just stepped from the pages of a magazine. Jessica stared after him, hopelessly mesmerized.

"Wait a minute," Cara protested, tugging at her arm. "You never did finish telling me about Ken and Ms. D—"

But Jessica had already forgotten about Ms. Dalton. She had Bruce in her sights, and like a bullet homing toward the target, she was dashing ahead to catch up with him.

Three

"Well, well, if it isn't Little Bo-Peep," drawled Bruce as Jessica fell in step beside him. He raked her over with a flick of his heavy-lidded blue eyes. "Lost any sheep lately?"

Jessica laughed as if it were the funniest joke in the world. Bruce Patman could recite the Gettysburg Address in pig latin and have all the girls in school hanging on his every word.

"I don't know what you're talking about, Bruce," she parried, fluttering her lashes at him. "I'm practically the loneliest girl in the whole school. Would you believe I don't even have a date for the dance yet?"

"I'll bet Egbert would take you. I hear he's really got the hots for you."

Jessica made a disgusted noise. "He's the last

boy on earth I'd want to go with! I mean, honestly, he's like some kind of—of—cartoon!"

Bruce chuckled. "Sure, old Scooby-Doo. Winston's for you, though."

"Oh, he's nice enough, but—well, you *know* what I mean." Jessica rolled her eyes in an expression meant to communicate that Winston was utterly hopeless.

Bruce laughed. "Yeah, I think I do, Jessica."

She felt his gaze travel over her as if sizing her up to see if she was his type. Apparently she met his approval, for his mouth curled up in a slow smile that sent Jessica's pulse pounding out of control. *She* had always known she was Bruce's type. Was he finally getting around to figuring it out as well?

She ran the tip of her tongue over her lips, wondering what it would be like when Bruce got around to kissing her. When, not if. The word "if" simply wasn't part of Jessica's vocabulary.

They were at the top of the stairs, and Jessica cast about wildly for some excuse to keep him from leaving. And then inspiration struck. She reached up, checking to see if her necklace—one of a pair of matching gold lavalieres their parents had given the twins on their sixteenth birthday—was under her sweater. It was.

"Oh!" she gasped. "My necklace! It must have fallen off on the stairs just now. Bruce, you've got to help me find it. My parents would absolutely murder me if I lost it. They practically went into debt for life to get it for me!"

Bruce cast an idle glance down the milling staircase. "I don't see it. But, listen, love, I'm sure it'll turn up. I've got to split. Catch you later." He was gone, leaving Jessica to gape after him in frustrated astonishment.

"Did I hear you say you lost your necklace?"

She turned to the voice behind her. There stood Winston Egbert, grinning foolishly and turning red to the tips of his ears.

She sighed. "Uh, yeah, but it's no big deal. I can look for it later."

"Gosh, Jessica, I don't mind helping you look," he gushed. "I'm good at finding things. My friends call me Sherlock Holmes. Once I even found a stamp my brother thought he'd lost out of his collection. You'd never guess in a million years where I found it. Sticking to the bottom of my shoe, that's where! I'll bet that's the last place in the world anyone else would've looked, huh?"

He advanced toward her just as Jessica was trying to step around him. "Ooops, sorry!" Winston blushed an even deeper shade of red. "I didn't mean to step on your toe. Are you OK?"

Jessica winced. Force of habit made her flash a dimpled smile anyway, in spite of her annoyance. "Thanks, Winston, but like I said, it's no big deal. I'm late for class."

"Sure, Jessica," he said, disappointment scrawled all over his face. "I guess I'll see you later, huh?"

The last sight she had as she rushed off down the corridor was of Winston Egbert down on his hands and knees, scouring the stairway for a nonexistent necklace.

Jessica arrived home from school in a black mood. Just when she'd come close to thinking Bruce might be interested in her, he'd done a complete turnabout, practically kicking her in the teeth. Now she was more hopelessly confused about him than ever. She simply *had* to find a way to get him. She remembered how his eyes had traveled over her—he certainly hadn't taken any shortcuts. Jessica warmed, just thinking about it. Maybe there really *was* a chance after all.

"Where's Liz?" she asked her mother, who was home from work early and was washing a head of lettuce.

"I think she's with Enid. Something about an art project. Posters for the dance, I believe."

Trim, tanned Alice Wakefield could easily have been mistaken for the twins' older sister. They shared the same beautiful all-American looks, down to the honey-colored hair that now swished softly about Alice Wakefield's shoulders as she bustled about the spacious, Spanish-tiled kitchen.

"Enid!" Jessica spat with exaggerated scorn. "Ugh! How can any sister of mine hang around with such a creepy little nerd?"

Mrs. Wakefield turned to give Jessica a gently reproving look. "I don't know how you can say that, Jess. Enid's a very nice girl. She and Liz seem to have a lot in common."

"Yeah, that's because she's turning herself into some kind of Liz-clone. It's positively revolting! She's always over here. Doesn't she have a home of her own?"

Alice Wakefield smiled as she patted the lettuce leaves dry. "Sounds like a slight case of the green-eyed monster to me."

"Me? Jealous of Enid Rollins?" Jessica made a gagging sound. "How could any mother say such a hideous thing to her own daughter?"

"Maybe because it's true," her mother suggested pleasantly.

"Mom!"

"Well, Liz *has* been spending a lot of time with Enid. You certainly don't see her as much as you used to."

"It's her business if she wants to associate with creeps, not mine. I mean, if *she* doesn't mind ruining her reputation by running around with that twerp, why should I care?"

"Good question. Honey, would you hand me the potato peeler out of the second drawer? That's it. Did I tell you Steve is coming home and bringing Tricia over for dinner tonight?"

30

Tricia Martin was her brother Steven's girl-friend. Although he lived in a dorm at the state university which was in a nearby town, he came home a lot, mostly because of Tricia. Most of the time Jessica was horrified that her very own brother was dating a girl from one of the worst families in town. But at the moment she was too preoccupied with thoughts of the social suicide Elizabeth was committing to give it half a second's notice.

"Liz can see who she wants," Jessica repeated. She scowled as she reached into the basket of cherry tomatoes on the sink and popped one into her mouth.

"Right."

"She can make friends with a one-eyed hippo-potamus for all I care."

"That's very open-minded of you. Don't eat all the tomatoes, Jess. Save a few for the salad."

"She can hang out with *ten* one-eyed hippos if that's what she wants to do. It's positively none of my business."

"I agree completely."

"If she'd rather be with Enid Rollins than me, why should it bother me? I have tons more friends than Liz does anyway. After all, I was the one who brought Enid home in the first place."

Jessica didn't like to admit it, but it was true. Enid had preferred Elizabeth's company to her own. To Jessica that was simply unforgivable.

She burst into tears. Darn Enid Rollins, she

31

thought. Darn Bruce Patman, too. She didn't need either of them. Everyone knew that she could get practically anyone to follow her simply by lifting her finger. Was it her fault that Enid and Bruce were blind to her charms?

Alice Wakefield laid a comforting hand on Jessica's shoulder. She was used to such tempests from her younger daughter (younger than Elizabeth by four minutes). From the time she was an infant, they had been as frequent, and usually as short-lived, as clouds passing in front of the sun.

"Don't worry, honey," she said. "No one could ever replace you as far as Liz is concerned."

"I should hope not!" Jessica stormed. "I'm the best friend Lizzie's got!"

"Then what are you getting so worked up about?"

"Nothing. Absolutely *nothing!*" She bit into another tomato and ended up squirting a red jet of juice and seeds down the front of her very favorite pink angora sweater.

"Ruined!" Jessica shrieked. "It's ruined for good!"

Mrs. Wakefield sighed as she handed her daughter the sponge. "Well, in that case, I suppose we could always have it for dinner, since that was the last tomato."

In a rage Jessica fled upstairs. She headed straight for Elizabeth's room and flung herself down on the bed. She preferred her sister's room to her own since it was always much neater. The Hershey Bar was what she called her room, due to its chocolate-colored walls. And it looked, in Elizabeth's immortal words, "like a cross between a mud-wrestling pit and the bargain table at K-Mart."

It wasn't fair, Jessica fumed. Elizabeth was going to the dance with Todd Wilkins. Even Enid had a date—with Ronnie Edwards, who was so blinded by love that as head of the dance committee, he'd probably swing a million votes her way. Ignoring the fact that she could have had her pick from any one of half a dozen boys if she'd wanted, Jessica refused to be consoled.

Then, out of the corner of one wet eye, she glimpsed a piece of paper sticking out from under the bed. It looked like a letter. Being naturally curious—and having absolutely zero scruples when it came to reading other people's mail—she snatched it up.

"Dear Enid," she read with a sudden, voracious interest. "Been so down lately. I can't seem to get my head on straight the way you have. I can't stop thinking about the past and trying to figure out how it all snowballed so quickly. It's like the time we took all those bennies, and before we knew it we were cooking along in the GTO doing eighty or ninety. . . ."

A smile crept slowly across Jessica's features as a plan shaped itself in her mind. She folded the letter, tucking it carefully into the back pocket of her jeans. She would have to put it back, of course, before Elizabeth discovered it was missing, but that was no problem.

Whistling under her breath, Jessica started back downstairs, heading for her father's den, where he kept a small Xerox machine for copying legal documents.

Four

"What is it with Ronnie and Enid?" Todd asked. "Are they having some kind of a fight?"

Todd and Elizabeth spoke in hushed tones while waiting for Ronnie and Enid to return to their seats with the popcorn. The two couples often double-dated, and the Valley Cinema was a favorite hangout. They'd always had a good time together in the past, but that night Elizabeth, too, noticed that something was off.

"Ronnie does seem to be acting strange," she admitted.

She didn't want him to know how truly worried she was for Enid, worried that somehow Ronnie might have found out her secret. She'd promised Enid she wouldn't tell, and that meant Todd, too, even though he was her boyfriend and she felt closer to him than anyone else.

Elizabeth looked over at Todd, more grateful than ever that he was hers—despite all the devious plots Jessica had cooked up in the beginning to keep them apart. Jessica had wanted him for herself, and Elizabeth could certainly see why. Todd was one of the best-looking boys at Sweet Valley High, besides being its hottest basketball star. He was tall and lean, with brown hair that curled down over his forehead and the kind of deep, coffee-colored eyes you could drown in. But the best thing about him was that he didn't give a darn whether he was popular or not. He was friendly with whomever he wanted to be friendly with, and he avoided people he considered snobs, no matter how popular they might be. In that way he and Elizabeth were alike. And she knew that she could tell him anything that was bothering her and he would have understood.

"Did you notice he didn't hold her hand during the movie?" Todd noted, giving Elizabeth's hand a reassuring squeeze. "Seemed kind of funny, since he's usually all over her."

She nodded. "Poor Enid. She really looked upset."

"I just hope Ronnie's not on one of his jealousy trips again. Remember the time he got mad at her for talking to that guy at Guido's?"

"All she was trying to do was make sure he didn't put anchovies on her pizza."

"It's crazy," Todd said, shaking his head. "If you love someone, you should trust him. Or her. Seems pretty dumb to get all worked up over nothing when you could be having a good time."

"Like us, you mean?" Elizabeth leaned close and brushed the side of his neck with her lips.

Todd kissed her softly in response.

She felt a tightening in her chest as she imagined what it would be like to lose Todd. Her heart went out to Enid, who had a thousand times more reason to worry.

"I hope Enid's all right," she said when she spotted Ronnie making his way down the aisle— alone. "Maybe I should go up and check."

She found Enid in the bathroom, dabbing at her eyes with a paper towel.

"Enid, what's wrong?" Elizabeth asked.

Enid shook her head. "I—I don't know. Ronnie's been acting like a different person all night. It's like he's a million miles away." Her eyes held a tortured expression. "Oh, Liz, do you think he knows?"

"Maybe it's something else," Elizabeth suggested not too hopefully. "A family problem. You mentioned his parents were divorced. . . ."

"Because his mother was fooling around with another man," Enid supplied bitterly.

"I'm sure it's not easy for him, living alone with just his father. Maybe they're not getting along. You really should talk to him, Enid. It might be something *he's* afraid to tell you."

"Yeah, like he wants to break up, only he's afraid I won't give him back his frat pin."

"Ronnie wouldn't do that. He loves you." But even as she said it, Elizabeth didn't feel very sure.

"To Ronnie, loving someone means absolute faithfulness," Enid said. "If he suspected for one second that I'd been writing to George, it would be the end. He'd never forgive me."

Anyone that inflexible didn't deserve someone as nice as Enid, Elizabeth thought.

"Don't worry," she said. "I'm the only one who knows about the letters. And even if he found out about the other stuff, it all happened way before you met him. He can't hold that against you, can he? It wouldn't be fair."

"Who ever said love was fair?" asked Enid, blowing loudly into a tissue.

She quickly fixed her makeup, then gave her shiny brown hair such a vigorous brushing that it flew up around her head in a crackle of electricity. She squared her shoulders as she gave her reflection a final inspection.

"Maybe I'm just imagining things," she said in a small voice. "Maybe Ronnie's just in a bad mood."

Elizabeth hoped she was right.

*   *   *

Riding home after they'd dropped off Elizabeth and Todd, Enid felt as if the gap between the bucket seats of Ronnie's Toyota had suddenly become the Continental Divide. She'd been hoping his silence was due to the fact that he felt uncomfortable about talking in front of Elizabeth and Todd, but he was acting just as distant now that they were gone.

"Where are we going?" she asked him when they passed the turnoff for her street.

"I thought we could park for a while," Ronnie replied in a neutral tone.

Glancing at his profile, silhouetted against the amber glow of a streetlight, Enid felt a surge of hope. He wanted to be with her after all! She longed to reach over and thread her fingers through the curly, reddish-brown hair at the nape of his neck, but she resisted the impulse. Even though it was clear he wanted to be with her, she still sensed something was wrong.

Ronnie found a place up on Miller's Point, a favorite Sweet Valley parking spot that overlooked the town. Already there were four or five other cars parked, and judging from the steaminess of their windows, they'd been there awhile.

Ronnie didn't waste any time. He lunged at Enid immediately after he switched off the engine, kissing her so roughly she was left gasping for breath.

"Hey, what's the big hurry?" She attempted

to make light of it, even though she was trembling when she'd finally managed to untangle herself from his crushing embrace.

Enid felt a growing sense of alarm. Ronnie had never acted like this before! Usually he was gentle, never pushing things beyond the limits she set. Tonight he was acting—uncontrollable. Something was terribly wrong.

"Sorry," he muttered. He sat back and began fiddling with the tape deck.

Loud, throbbing rock music filled the car. Usually, he chose something soft and romantic, but this evening he obviously wasn't in that sort of mood.

"Ronnie—what is it?" she blurted. "What's wrong?"

He drummed his fingers nervously against the steering wheel, unable to meet her eyes. "Uh, well, I didn't want to tell you, but it's about the dance. I, uh—"

Enid felt as if her heart were suspended in midair. "What about the dance?"

"I'm not sure I'll be able to make it. You see, I might have to work for my dad that night. He's going out of town, and he really needs someone to look after the store."

"Gee, Ronnie, that's too bad." Enid felt sick.

Ronnie's father owned a small all-night supermarket, but Enid knew he could have called upon any one of half a dozen people to replace him. Ronnie hadn't even bothered to come up with a halfway decent excuse for dumping her. A hot, pricking sensation behind her eyes warned that tears were dangerously close. She fought them. She was determined to hold her head up, not to let him see how much he was hurting her.

"Yeah, well, I'm sorry about it, Enid, but you know how it goes sometimes. Anyway, I'll let you know for sure one way or another in a couple of days."

He thinks he's letting me down easy, Enid thought. Easy? This was agony. She'd imagined this scene so many times, but now that it was actually happening, it didn't seem real. Enid shivered, suddenly feeling very cold and alone. She longed for the warmth of Ronnie's arms around her, even if he was acting strangely. She tried once again to make believe it was only her imagination. She wanted to put everything back the way it was, to pretend Ronnie loved her the same as always. In her desperation Enid felt herself begin to weaken as Ronnie's arms tightened around her again, his lips moving against hers with a hard, unrelenting pressure. But something inside her wouldn't let go. *No, this isn't the way!* She stiffened and pulled back.

"Ronnie—please. Can't we just sit here and talk for a while?" she pleaded.

"What about?" He sounded cold and defensive.

"Uh—" It was on the tip of her tongue to tell him right then and there, to blurt out everything

that had been building up since the first time
she'd gone out with him. But somehow she just
couldn't get the words unstuck from her throat.
"I don't know. Just talk. Heard anything interesting around school lately?"

"You mean the latest about Ken Matthews
and Ms. Dalton?"

"What about them?" she asked.

"I can't believe you haven't heard. It's all
over school. They're having an affair."

"I don't believe it!" For a moment Enid forgot
her own despair. "Ms. Dalton wouldn't do a
thing like that!"

"How do you know?" Ronnie challenged.
"People do crummy things all the time."

"I just can't believe she would—"

"Be interested in Ken?" he supplied, sneering.
"I would. A lot of people are two-faced, especially
when it comes to love."

Now it was Enid's turn to get angry. "Wait a
minute. You don't know anything about it. Who
told you all this, anyway? Did anyone actually
see them together?"

The image of refined Ms. Dalton in the arms
of some high school jock simply refused to come.
Of course, Enid was prejudiced. Ms. Dalton
happened to be her favorite teacher. Once when
Enid had come to school practically in tears
over a problem she was having with her mother,
Ms. Dalton had taken her aside after class and
comforted her. Ever since then, she'd found it

easy to talk to her and had fallen into the habit of stopping by after school when something was bothering her. Ms. Dalton never seemed to mind, and always made time for her. The truth was, Enid didn't *want* to believe she was capable of anything so awful.

"Who cares?" Ronnie said carelessly. "It's probably true, anyway."

He pulled her against him. Even his face felt rough against her skin as he kissed her. When she tried to pull away, he only held on tighter.

Finally Enid managed to wrench free of his grasp. She twisted away from him, facing the window so he wouldn't see that she was crying. Hot tears dripped onto the hands she held tightly clenched in her lap, so tightly her fingernails dug into her palms.

"What's the matter?" Ronnie growled. "I don't rate up there with old Georgie-boy? You're not going to give me any of the same stuff you're giving him?"

Enid gasped as if she'd been punched in the stomach. "How—how do you know about George?"

"What difference does it make? The fact is, I *know*." His eyes narrowed with scorn. "I know a lot of things about you I didn't know before, Enid. I know, for instance, that you're not as pure as you'd like me to believe."

"Ronnie, don't . . ." Enid put her hands over

her face, unable to meet his eyes. He hated her. He really *hated* her.

He pried them away, forcing her to look at him. His fingers bit into her wrists, cutting off the circulation. "You've been deceiving me," he hissed, "I know all about it!"

"Ronnie, please, you don't understand! Let me explain!"

"Oh, I understand, all right. A lot of things. Like what an idiot I've been. All this time you were pretending to be in love with me, you were carrying on with someone else behind my back, writing him love letters. How could I have been so stupid!"

Enid felt as if her throat were being squeezed in a giant fist. She struggled against her sobs.

"Ronnie, please listen. George and I are only friends. It's true we used to date, but that was a long time ago. You've got to believe me!"

"Why *should* I believe you? You've been lying to me all along. Acting like Miss Goody Two-Shoes when the truth is you were hot and heavy with George and who knows who else."

Finally he'd gone too far. Giving a cry of anger, Enid yanked her wrists from his grasp. "OK, if that's what you want to think! It's obvious you don't even care what my side is! Why can't you *trust* me just a little?"

"Trust?" Ronnie sneered. "Isn't that kind of a funny word for you to use, Enid? Especially when all the time I was trusting you, you were knifing me in the back. Forget it, baby. I'm taking you home."

Enid couldn't believe she was hearing Ronnie speak to her like this. It was as if he'd turned from Dr. Jekyll into Mr. Hyde. The nightmare she'd dreaded for so long was coming true, and it was even more awful than anything she could have imagined.

Ronnie drove her home in stony silence while she huddled in the seat beside him, desperately holding in her sobs. One thought scuttered through her mind like a rat in a maze, doubling the blow of betrayal she felt:

The letters. Liz must have told him about the letters.

Five

Elizabeth had never seen her sister in such a good mood. Jessica was making her positively dizzy, flying around the room like a hyperactive bumblebee as she got ready to spend Saturday night out with Cara.

"What do you think?" Jessica held up her ribbed burgundy sweater dress. "With that new belt I bought at the mall last month?"

"You're certainly going to a lot of trouble fixing yourself up just to go somewhere with Cara," Elizabeth observed. "What's up?"

"That's for me to know—and you, big sister, to find out," Jessica replied, smiling mysteriously.

She hummed as she launched into the task of untangling her hair from the jumble of electric curlers that sprouted from her head. Elizabeth knew her game, though, and she wasn't going to play it.

She yawned. "Well, have fun—whatever it is."

Jessica stopped to glare at her sister's reflection in the mirror. "Aren't you even the tiniest bit curious about where we're going?"

"Not really." Elizabeth yawned again.

"You mean you're not even going to try to guess?" Jessica's lower lip edged out in a tiny pout.

"OK. Let me see . . . you've been invited to a White House reception and your fairy godmother is getting ready to turn a zucchini from Mom's garden into a jet."

Jessica threw a hairbrush at her sister, missing her by several inches. "Very funny." She was trying very hard not to laugh.

"OK." Elizabeth giggled. "I give up. Where *are* you going?"

"To a party at Lila's. You could've been invited, too, if you tried a little harder to be friends with Lila."

Elizabeth shrugged. "Why should I? I think she's a phony."

"No phonier than some of *your* friends," Jessica shot back. "I won't mention any names, but I think you know who I mean. Her first initial is E—and I'm not talking about E.T., either."

"No comment," said Elizabeth. It bothered

her that Jessica was so determined to dislike Enid, but she knew if her sister guessed what she was feeling, she'd never let up. "Anyway, I wouldn't go to Lila's party even if I was invited. Face it, Jess, the Fowlers are snobs. I guess it comes from getting rich practically overnight."

"I don't care if their money grows on trees," Jessica said. "The point is, they know all the right people. Everybody who's anybody will be at that party."

"You mean like Bruce Patman, Bruce Patman, and Bruce Patman?" Elizabeth couldn't resist teasing her.

"You can joke about it all you like," Jessica said. "As a matter of fact, he is going to be there, and I'm making sure he notices me. So what do you think? Is the sweater dress OK? You don't think it makes me look fat, do you?"

"Yes and no."

"What?" Jessica screeched as if she'd just been mortally wounded. She whirled to face her sister. "How dare you suggest I'm fat? We weigh exactly the same, for your information!"

"Cool it, Jess. I meant yes, the dress is fine, and no, it doesn't make you look fat."

"That's better." Jessica switched back to her usual ultra-charming self, flashing Elizabeth a brilliant smile.

She yanked the last curler from her hair, letting loose a mass of golden ringlets. Curly hair was the one thing Jessica regretted not having been blessed with.

Elizabeth went back to her room and to the book she was reading, but she couldn't seem to concentrate. She was thinking about Enid, worrying over the fact that she hadn't called. It had been a whole twenty-four hours since their double-date—a record for silence where Enid was concerned. Especially since she had to know that Elizabeth was dying to find out how her confrontation with Ronnie had come out. She'd tried calling Enid herself, but both times her mother had said that she was too busy to come to the phone.

Something strange was going on.

Elizabeth decided she would try calling once more, and if Enid wouldn't come to the phone, then she was going over there herself to see what was the matter. Had Ronnie broken up with Enid? she wondered anxiously. Was Enid angry with her for advising her to be truthful with him?

This time Enid answered the phone herself—though Elizabeth scarcely recognized her voice. She sounded so cold and distant.

"Are you OK, Enid?" Elizabeth asked. "You sound funny, like you have a cold or something."

"I'm all right."

"You don't *sound* all right. Aren't you going to tell me what happened last night?"

Enid laughed, but it was a dry, harsh sound. "I'm surprised you have to ask, Liz. I should think it would be pretty obvious to you."

"What are you talking about? Enid, hey, it's me, Liz. What's going on with you? Look, I'm sorry if I told you to level with Ronnie. Was he upset when you told him? Is that it?"

"*Upset?*" Enid choked. "Yeah, I'd say he was upset, all right. Only I wasn't the one who told him."

"So he knows about the police record. Big deal. He'll get over it in a day or two. After all, it happened such a long time ago. It has nothing to do with you and Ronnie now."

"He knows about the letters."

Elizabeth gasped. "How could he have found out? You and I were the only ones who knew!"

"That's right," Enid replied icily.

"Oh, Enid, you couldn't possibly think—"

"*What am I supposed to think?*" Enid was crying now. "*You* tell *me.*"

"I—I don't know." Elizabeth was too stunned to think straight. "But, Enid, you've got to believe I never—"

"Why should I believe you? You're the only one who knew about those letters. *The only one.* I confided in you. It *had* to be you. Oh, Liz, how could you do this to me?"

"Enid, please—"

Before she could finish, Enid had slammed

the phone down. For a long time Elizabeth refused to believe what had just happened. She sat listening to the empty hum of the dial tone for several moments before slowly lowering the receiver.

"Who was that?" Jessica asked from behind her. "It sounded like you were having some kind of argument."

"Enid," Elizabeth replied, her eyes welling with tears. "It was Enid."

Jessica made a face. "What did *she* want? Wait a minute, don't tell me, let me guess—she couldn't walk from the living room into the kitchen without asking your opinion about it first, right?"

"Jessica, stop it!" Elizabeth snapped. "It's not funny. Enid was really upset. She and Ronnie have broken up—and she thinks it's all my fault."

In a burst, she confided in her sister about what had happened. Jessica rushed to her sister and threw her arms around her.

"It's so unfair! How could she accuse you of such a thing? There must have been some mistake. Enid probably let it slip out about the letters herself, and now she wants to blame someone else. I always knew she was just using you, Lizzie. I saw right through her from the very beginning. You're better off without her."

Elizabeth disentangled herself from her sister's

suffocating embrace. "I'm sure Enid didn't mean all those things she said. She was just upset about breaking up with Ronnie. It must have been pretty awful for her."

"What about you? Look what she's putting *you* through!"

"I'll survive. But I'm worried about Enid."

"For heaven's sake, Liz, are you trying to win the Nobel Peace Prize or something? Don't you ever fight back?"

"All I want to do is straighten out this whole mess. I just hope Enid will listen to me! I have a feeling if I called back right now, she'd only hang up on me again."

"So wait until you see her on Monday. Let her wait until then."

Elizabeth chewed her lip thoughtfully. "Maybe it would be better to wait. I don't think she's in the mood to listen to anybody right now. Poor Enid! I can't believe Ronnie would do this to her over a few crummy letters from a boy she's not even dating anymore."

"Don't you see? It's the principle of the thing. How could he ever trust her again, knowing how she'd covered up the truth? Honestly, Liz, I think it's better Ronnie *did* find out. Whoever told him about the letters was doing him a big favor."

"But *who?*" cried Elizabeth. "*Who* would have done such a hideous thing?"

She looked up to ask Jessica's opinion, but her twin was off again in a whirlwind of preparation for the party. Clearly, the subject was beginning to bore her.

Six

Lila pressed a glass of red wine into Jessica's hand. "Try some," she said and giggled. "It's really good French stuff. I snitched a couple of bottles from my dad's wine cellar, but I'm sure he won't notice. He's got loads of it."

Jessica took a tentative sip. She felt very elegant, sitting there drinking wine at the Fowler mansion. Everything about Fowler Crest was elegant, from the magnificently landscaped grounds to the uniformed maid who had taken their coats when they had come in. It made Jessica's own comfortable split-level house seem like a shack in comparison.

"I can't believe your father lets you have parties like this when he's not here," she said to Lila.

A tiny frown creased Lila's forehead. "Well—I didn't exactly tell him I was having a party. I just said I was having a few friends over. What he doesn't know won't hurt him, right? Besides, it's his own fault for not spending more time at home. If he wasn't so busy running around with Ms. Dalton . . ." Her voice trailed off, and her frown darkened to a scowl.

"Speaking of Ms. D—" Cara began.

"Who *hasn't* been talking about her?" Jessica broke in impatiently. "Frankly, I'm sick of it. Can't anyone talk about anything else?" Jessica quickly grew bored with gossip that didn't directly concern her. It seemed that the girls of Pi Beta Alpha, the sorority that Jessica, Cara, and Lila belonged to, could talk of nothing else.

"Have you heard the news about Ronnie and Enid?" Cara whispered, catching sight of Ronnie standing over by the fireplace. Gossip was gossip, as far as she was concerned. It didn't much matter who the target was.

"Knowing you," Dana Larson put in as she glided up to the bar, "you probably found out about it before Enid did." She held out her empty glass to Lila. "Just Pepsi for me. Got to protect my pipes."

Dana was lead singer for The Droids, Sweet Valley High's answer to the Rolling Stones. They had a reputation for being pretty wild, but most of it was just conjecture. Not many outsiders knew what went on in the smoky confines of

55

Max Dellon's basement, where they held their practice sessions. As for Dana, she was fairly straight underneath the outrageous clothes she wore. Tonight she was decked out in tight black velvet jeans, a pair of sparkly pink leg warmers, and a purple satin blouse.

Cara nudged Jessica in the ribs. "Ronnie doesn't look too happy. Why don't you go over there and cheer him up?"

"No, thanks, I'm saving myself." She perched on a stool and crossed her legs, making sure her hemline was just far enough above her knee to make it interesting.

"If you mean Bruce, you can forget it," said Lila. "He's not coming."

"What?" Jessica nearly fell off her stool.

"He called at the last minute to tell me he was going to some bash at the college. You know Bruce, always hanging around with older women."

Jessica's heart plummeted into her shoes—Elizabeth's shoes, actually, which she'd borrowed. After all the trouble she'd gone to, Bruce didn't even have the decency to show up! She knew that if he'd just give her half a chance, she could have him wrapped around her little finger. The tricky part was getting him there in the first place. She could see it wasn't going to be easy, but Jessica didn't discourage easily, either. She was already halfway there—thanks to Enid's letter.

Jessica squelched a tiny twinge of guilt as she remembered how upset Elizabeth had been. After all, how was *she* to know Enid would blame her sister? Really, the whole thing was Enid's fault from start to finish. People who left letters lying around for anyone in the world to see were just begging for trouble.

"The girl he's taking to the dance is *nineteen*, for heaven's sake," Lila went on. "I can't believe anyone that *ancient* would want to hang out at a high school dance."

Jessica scarcely heard the rest of what Lila was saying. Her mind was stuck like a broken record on those first words: *The girl he's taking to the dance . . .*

She gulped down half her glass of wine, gasping as it burned a fiery path down her throat. Nevertheless, she refused to surrender. The battle was not lost yet. It just called for a little new strategy and a fresh round of ammunition.

"This isn't going to be just *any* high school dance," Dana said. "After all, when you've got the greatest band around . . ."

Jessica tuned out the conversation. With her eye on Ronnie, she slithered off her stool and made straight for her prey.

"Hey, heartbreaker," she drawled, linking her arm through Ronnie's. "Why don't you try cheering up? This is supposed to be a party. Aren't you having a good time?"

"Yeah," he snarled into his drink. "I'm having a ball."

"Well, you look like someone with a terminal case of the blahs. Come on, I know a terrific cure—let's dance."

"Thanks, Jessica, but I think I'll pass. I'm not really in the mood. Maybe later."

Jessica dropped her flirtatious pose and changed tactics. "Maybe you should have brought Enid," she suggested sweetly. "It's obvious you're miserable without her."

"Enid!" He looked as if she'd just injected him with poison. "No thanks, I'd be better off with Benedict Arnold."

Jessica cleverly jumped to Enid's defense.

"You shouldn't be so hard on her," she said. "After all, everyone makes mistakes. I suppose she's sorry, I'm sure there's no reason for you to hate her for life."

"Yeah, well, I happen to know Enid's not sorry at all. I even have written proof. Someone left a copy of a letter in my locker that some creep named George wrote to Enid."

Jessica pretended total innocence. "Liz did mention that George had been writing to Enid, but you know how those things are," she said. "When you're *involved* with someone the way Enid was with George, it's hard to break it off just like that."

"She's been writing to that jerk for two years!"

"Mmmm," Jessica conceded, taking a ladylike

sip of her wine. "That certainly does *seem* devoted. But just remember, appearances can be deceiving."

"Oh, I get the picture, all right," Ronnie said. "Look, Jessica, I appreciate what you're trying to do. It's nice of you to try to help Enid, but it's not going to work. It's over between us."

"What about the dance? Enid is up for queen."

"She should've thought of that before. It's her problem now, not mine. I'm sure she won't have any trouble conning some other poor jerk into taking her."

"What about you, though?" Jessica flashed him a smile oozing with sympathy.

He shrugged. "I'll probably just stay home. It's too late to get another date now."

"Well, what a coincidence!" she cried, clapping a hand over her mouth. "Would you believe I don't have a date, either?"

Several other boys had asked her, of course, but she'd turned them all down. She'd been saving herself for Bruce, and now it was too late—they all had other dates. And the dance was only a week away.

"Since *you* don't have a date and *I* don't have a date," she suggested, "why don't we go together?"

He looked at her as if she'd just suggested he carry her cross-country on his back. "I, uh, gosh, Jessica . . ."

"Just as friends, of course."

59

"It does make sense," he agreed then.

"Well, there's certainly no point in sitting home and getting even more depressed, is there?" she asked.

"I guess not." He looked slightly bewildered, like someone who'd been picked up by a tornado and dropped in a foreign land.

Jessica turned her most radiant smile on him. Sliding her hand down his arm, she laced her fingers through his. She led him over to the dance area, where several couples had gone into body lock.

"Oh, by the way, Ronnie," she cooed, "I'm allergic to gardenias, but I absolutely *adore* orchids. Just don't get me a pink one—I'll be wearing a red dress."

Seven

Elizabeth arrived at school Monday morning to find her problem with Enid overshadowed by an item of gossip that had taken off and, in the last week, spread rapidly.

Practically everyone at Sweet Valley High was buzzing about The Affair—the one supposedly going on between Ms. Dalton and Ken Matthews.

"I don't buy it for one minute," Elizabeth told Caroline Pearce, a member of Pi Beta Alpha sorority, after first period as they stood outside the French classroom.

They were waiting for Ms. Dalton to arrive and unlock the door. Elizabeth couldn't remember her ever having been late before. But then everything about Ms. Dalton had seemed not quite right this past week. In class she was nervous and distracted. Elizabeth had noticed dark circles under her eyes, as if she hadn't been sleeping well.

"I refuse to believe she's fooling around with Ken," Elizabeth went on. "It just doesn't make sense. Why would anyone as together as Ms. Dalton be interested in a *kid?*"

"Ken Matthews isn't exactly a kid," Caroline countered, primly tossing her impossibly neat red hair. Aside from Cara, she was probably the biggest gossip around—and the one person Jessica and Elizabeth could agree on disliking. "Besides, everyone knows she's tutoring him. The question is, *what* is she tutoring him in?"

"It's the law of human nature," put in Olivia Davidson, who worked with Elizabeth on the paper and was known for her liberal views on every subject from nuclear war to organic food. She was especially big these days on women's rights. "A woman doesn't reach her peak until she's in her thirties. Men are practically burned out by then. So it makes sense, really, when you think about it. Though I still can't imagine Ms. Dalton and Ken."

"What makes sense?" asked Lois Waller.

"For an older woman to be attracted to a younger man." Caroline filled her in.

"Maybe," said Elizabeth, "but I still don't think it's true in this case. Ms. Dalton is our teacher. She wouldn't do something as unprincipled as that, even if she wanted to."

"God, Liz, you are soooo naive," Caroline drawled. "Anyway, that's what makes it so perfect. It's so disgustingly tacky."

"I talked to someone in Ms. Dalton's first-period French class who told me Ms. Dalton seemed upset, like she was on the verge of tears or something."

"Maybe someone in her family just died," suggested Lois, a shaggy-haired girl with oversized glasses which kept slipping down her nose as she talked.

"Or maybe someone's about to get fired," sneered Caroline. "My father plays golf with old Chrome Dome and says he's practically Billy Graham when it comes to stuff like teachers' morals."

"I'm with Liz," Olivia argued. "Ms. Dalton just doesn't seem like the type."

Guy Chesney, keyboard player for The Droids, skidded to a stop before them, whipping out a grubby pad and a pencil stub that looked as if it had been chewed by a pack of rats. His impish brown eyes were lit up with mischief. "I'm taking a poll," he said. "So far it's only one out of three in Ms. Dalton's favor. Goes to show, people always want to believe the worst. Me, I thrive on rumors."

"Has anyone bothered to ask Ms. Dalton whether it's true or not?" Elizabeth wondered.

"Why would she tell *us*?" Caroline replied,

looking horrified at the idea. "It's not exactly the kind of thing she'd want printed on the front page of *The Oracle*."

Guy laughed. "Sounds like a great idea to me. I'll bet it'd sell more copies than *Playboy*. Hey, maybe you could even staple in a fold-out of Ms. Dalton while you're at it."

All four girls eyed him with a drop-dead expression.

"OK, OK," he backed off. "It was just an idea. I mean, heck, any woman with a body like hers . . ." His voice trailed off when he saw he was only making it worse for himself.

At that moment the subject of their heated discussion arrived on the scene, putting an abrupt end to the conversation.

"*Bonjour*, class," Ms. Dalton greeted them as she unlocked the door.

She seemed more subdued than usual, and she was wearing a pair of very dark sunglasses—something Elizabeth had never seen her do before. A ripple of uneasiness edged its way up her spine. Suppose, just suppose, it *were* true. . . .

Ms. Dalton froze as she entered the classroom. Someone had scrawled on the blackboard in large block letters:

IF YOU DON'T KNOW WHAT A FRENCH KISS
IS,
ASK KEN MATTHEWS

Elizabeth gasped. She felt sick. But her reaction was nothing compared to Ms. Dalton's, who reeled back as if she'd been slapped, burst into tears, and rushed out into the corridor.

Elizabeth was still upset about what had happened in Ms. Dalton's classroom by the time she caught up with Enid at the end of third period, but she was determined to put a stop to this ridiculous business of not speaking to one another.

"It's no use avoiding me," said Elizabeth, blocking Enid's path as she attempted to brush past her. "Enid, we *have* to talk."

"I have nothing to say to you, Elizabeth Wakefield," Enid replied icily.

"Enid, you're my best friend. I would *never* betray you. You have to believe me. I swear I didn't tell anyone about those letters."

"The next thing you'll be telling me is that your room is bugged."

"Don't be ridiculous!" Elizabeth was starting to get a little angry herself. "Why can't you just trust me?"

"I *did* trust you, remember? Look where it got me. Thanks to you, my whole life is ruined!"

"Maybe if I talked to Ronnie . . ." Elizabeth began, desperate for any solution to heal this awful rift.

Enid's icy reserve cracked in a sudden flood

of fury. "Haven't you done enough talking?" she yelled. "Can't you just keep your big mouth shut?"

Elizabeth flinched, feeling the color drain from her face. With a choked cry, Enid whirled off in the opposite direction, her head down to hide the tears she couldn't stop from falling.

"Hi, Liz!" Cara called cheerily from her post by the water fountain, where the only thing she'd been drinking in was the sight of Elizabeth and Enid arguing.

By lunchtime it was all over school that Ronnie and Enid had broken up and that Elizabeth had something to do with it. Between Ms. Dalton and Enid, the gossip mongers of Sweet Valley High were in heaven.

"Don't worry," Jessica consoled her sister as they sat on the lawn eating their lunches. "You did everything you could. If Enid wants to be stubborn about it, you can't blame yourself."

"I just wish I didn't feel so helpless," Elizabeth said sadly, nibbling on a corn chip, even though she wasn't the least bit hungry.

"Maybe I should try talking to Enid myself," Jessica suggested sweetly.

"You? You don't even like her! Why should you?"

Jessica pretended to be hurt. "Jeez! Excuse me for breathing! I was only trying to help—you don't have to bite my head off. I just hate

66

Eight

It was obvious Enid was in no mood for talking, but Jessica wasn't about to let a little thing like that stand in her way. She quickened her step as she fell in beside Enid, blocking her attempt to make a rapid getaway.

"I know how you feel," Jessica gushed sympathetically. "Well, actually, I've never been dumped by anyone, but I can *imagine* what it's like. You must feel awful!"

Enid's lips tightened. "I'm sure Liz filled you in on all the gory details. Why doesn't she just take out an ad in *The Sweet Valley News*?"

"Oh, come on, Enid, don't be that way. Why shouldn't Liz tell me? I *am* her sister. I'm closer to her than anyone in the whole world."

"That's pretty obvious."

"You shouldn't be so hard on her," Jessica cajoled. "I'm *sure* she never meant to hurt you. You know how these things are."

Enid stopped to look at her. "No, I don't know how these things are," she answered coldly. "Unlike *some* people, I'm not in the habit of stabbing my friends in the back."

"You act as if Liz did it on purpose, for heaven's sake! I'm positive she didn't mean to tell Ronnie. It probably just slipped out."

"Just slipped out? Is that what she told you?" Enid's eyes narrowed.

"Well, uh, not exactly, but I—"

"Oh, stop it!" Enid snapped. "Stop trying to defend her. Nothing can excuse what she did!"

"If only you knew how upset Liz is over this whole thing."

"What about me? *I'm* the one who lost her boyfriend, remember? Don't tell me about upset! Liz doesn't know the meaning of the word. She's still got Todd and I've got . . . nothing." Enid choked on the last word.

"I wouldn't exactly say that, Enid. You've still got George."

"That's right. I've still got George. After all, we outcasts have to stick together, right?"

"I wouldn't go so far as to call you an outcast, Enid," Jessica replied generously. "Sure you made some mistakes, but don't worry, people aren't going to believe *everything* Ronnie's been saying about you."

Enid seemed to fold up before Jessica's eyes. Like a dress slipping from its hanger, she slumped down on a bench.

"What has Ronnie been saying about me?" she asked in a hoarse whisper.

Jessica slid a consoling arm about her shoulders. "Believe me, you wouldn't want to know. I couldn't even *repeat* half of it."

"Oh!" Enid buried her face in her hands. "I could just die!"

"It can't be all that bad," Jessica told her. "Look at the bright side. Now you don't have to hide in the closet anymore. It must be a relief not to wonder what people are whispering about you all the time."

"Yeah, now I *know* what they're whispering about me." Enid rose slowly, painfully, to her feet. "Thanks, Jessica, I know you're only trying to help, but you can tell Liz to forget it. If I live to be a hundred and ninety-nine, I'll never forgive her for this!"

"I think you're making a mistake, Enid," Jessica replied lightly.

Enid's mouth twisted in a bitter smile. "Yeah, well, it wouldn't be the first time."

This time Jessica made no attempt to stop her as she rushed off. Elizabeth was better off without Enid for a friend, she thought. Who knew what kind of trouble Elizabeth might get into if she hung around Enid long enough? In the long run, Jessica told herself, she was doing everyone a big favor.

Including herself.

And why not? Didn't she deserve to be happy as much as anyone?

A smile tugged at the corners of her mouth. Since Enid was no longer with Ronnie, she couldn't possibly get enough votes on her own to be chosen queen. Now that Enid was out of the running, Jessica could almost feel the delicious weight of the crown on her head.

"Watch out, Bruce Patman," she murmured under her breath. "Here I come!"

"Why would Ronnie Edwards be calling you?" Elizabeth asked later that evening as Jessica returned from a huddled conversation on the upstairs extension.

Elizabeth looked up from the paper on Shakespeare's *Julius Caesar* she was working on, then went back to it.

"*O, pardon me, thou bleeding piece of Enid,*" she unconsciously copied. She scratched out Enid's name and corrected it to "earth."

"I, uh, well—you might as well know." Jessica flopped down on the bed beside her. "I'm going to the dance with Ronnie."

"You're what?" Elizabeth's pen clattered to the floor.

"It wasn't easy convincing him. He was pretty angry. But I finally managed."

"Jessica, what on earth are you talking about? How can you even *think* of doing such a thing? It would absolutely kill Enid!"

Jessica's expression turned sulky. "Don't you see? I'm doing it *for* Enid. I felt so bad about botching things up with her this afternoon. So I decided to talk to Ronnie."

"What did he say?"

"He was still pretty upset, like I said. I could see it was going to be really hard to get those two back together."

"But you decided to do it, right?"

"What else could I do? He absolutely wasn't going to budge on his own, even after I told him how sorry Enid was and all."

"He's the one who should be sorry," Elizabeth muttered.

"So I figured the only way was for him to see Enid at the dance. If we could arrange to set them up for at least one dance, I'm sure everything will work itself out."

"True love conquers all?" Elizabeth remained skeptical. She was even more skeptical about why Jessica was doing all this, but she decided not to ask. "I'm not so sure it's the best idea in the world. Maybe we should just let them work it out on their own. Besides, I doubt if Enid is going to the dance now that Ronnie broke their date."

73

"In that case, you'll just have to find a way of talking her into it. I wouldn't want anyone to think I was going with Ronnie for my own selfish purposes." She looked positively horrified at the thought.

Elizabeth relented at the sincerity in her sister's tone. "I'm sorry, Jess," she said. "I know you're just trying to help."

"I'm doing it for *you*, Lizzie!" cried Jessica, giving Elizabeth's hand a warm squeeze.

"How does all this benefit me?"

"I just thought that if Enid and Ronnie got back together, then Enid wouldn't be so mad at you anymore."

"Ah, the mists are clearing."

"You don't need to get sarcastic—even though I know you're still furious at me for blowing it with Enid today."

"She took one look at me in gym class today and burst into tears," Elizabeth said miserably. "I felt like an ax murderer or something. Jess, what did you *say* to her?"

"Nothing much, really. Actually, it was Enid who did most of the talking. She said some *awful* things about you, Liz!"

"She did?" Elizabeth's heart sank.

"I could hardly believe my ears! You know, I think she's always been jealous of you, Lizzie. She was probably just waiting around for an excuse like this to pounce on you."

74

"I know Enid is angry with me, but somehow that just doesn't sound like her."

"Well, you *asked* me."

"I'm sorry I did, in that case."

"Hmphhh!" Jessica tossed her head in disdain. "That's the last time I ever try to do you a favor."

She leaped from the bed in a huff that lasted about thirty seconds—the time it took for her to plow through Elizabeth's closet.

"I *might* forgive you, if you'll loan me your beaded bag for the dance," she said.

"No way. I'm planning on using it myself."

"But you'll be wearing your green dress. It'll go so much better with mine. You can borrow Mom's gold purse. I'm sure she won't mind lending it to you. I mean, think of what a sacrifice I'm making by going at all. The least you could do is appreciate it."

Elizabeth sighed. "I guess the gold purse *would* look better with green."

Jessica blew her sister a hasty kiss as she dashed out of the room. "I've got to call Cara and see what she's going to wear."

Elizabeth was left to wonder why, if Jessica was doing her such a big favor, *she* was the one making all the sacrifices.

Nine

The next day Elizabeth broke down and confided in Mr. Collins. Besides being the faculty adviser for *The Oracle*, Roger Collins had become a sort of unofficial "Dear Abby" to the kids who worked with him. Of course, he resembled anyone *but* Abby—more like a taller Robert Redford, Elizabeth thought, with his crinkly blue eyes and ruggedly handsome features. Sometimes it was hard to keep her mind on what she was saying when she talked to him.

"Mmm, sounds like you've got a bit of a mystery on your hands," he said. "Seems to me the first step you have to take is figuring out why someone would want to tell Ronnie about those letters."

"Motivation, right?" Elizabeth's writer's mind

clicked into gear. "The trouble is, nobody else knew about those letters besides me."

"That's what Enid thinks. But somebody else must have known. What about this boy she was exchanging these letters with? Does he have any friends here at school?"

Elizabeth thought for a moment. "I suppose he could have told Winston Egbert." She knew they'd been friends from the age of about five, though Winston had kept far away from the trouble George had gotten himself into.

"It's a possibility. But even if Winston did know, I can't think of why he would have told Ronnie."

Mr. Collins smiled. "I'm sure he wouldn't have said anything to be malicious, but sometimes people tell secrets just to get attention."

Winston did have a tendency to be a blabbermouth, Elizabeth thought, but he would have had to go out of his way to tell Ronnie, someone he wasn't even friends with, about the letters. Still, she had to admit it was the best possibility so far.

"I suppose I could ask him," she said.

"That's using your head." Mr. Collins winked at her as if she'd thought it up all on her own. "I'm sure it'll turn out one way or another, Liz. Enid's hurting right now, and when people are hurt, they want someone to lash out at. Often it's someone they love."

"Why is that?"

"Because the people we love, who love us, are the ones who will forgive us later on when it all blows over."

Elizabeth looked at him, a slow smile flickering across her features. "How did you get to be so smart, Mr. Collins?"

He shrugged. "Remember, I've been around a few more years than you."

"Yes, Grandpa," she teased.

"Not *that* long." He laughed. "I've got a way to go yet before they put me out to pasture. Besides, how would all you goof-offs get along without me to crack the whip over you?"

"We'd probably turn this paper into *The National Enquirer*," Olivia interjected as she sailed past, bearing an armload of letters she'd collected from the box outside their office. "Honestly, you should *see* some of this garbage!"

Mr. Collins's expression darkened as he examined a few of the letters she'd dumped on his desk. "*This*," he said, jabbing his finger at an offending note, "is what I call malicious gossip. The worst kind, since it's totally unfounded. I spoke with Nora Dalton this morning in the teachers' lounge, and I can tell you she's pretty upset about all this talk. She's actually made herself sick over it. In fact, she looked so bad, I talked her into going home and getting some rest."

"I heard she even got some obscene phone calls at her apartment," Olivia said. "Gosh, I don't know what I'd do if it were me. How does she stand it?"

"The best way she knows how—by not giving it more credence than it deserves. I think we should all do the same." With one swoop, he swept the letters into the trash can.

Everyone suspected that Mr. Collins had a special interest in the pretty Ms. Dalton, so he had double the reason to be disturbed over what was happening. At least *he* trusted her, though, Elizabeth thought.

"I wonder how Kenny's taking it," she mused aloud.

"Nobody seems to know," Olivia answered. "He's been absent the past couple of days. There's a nasty rumor that he got mononucleosis from k—"

"That's enough!" In a rare show of temper, Mr. Collins slammed a book down on his desk. "Haven't you two got anything better to do than talk about this thing?"

Elizabeth blushed. Mr. Collins was right—the best way to deal with gossip was just to ignore it. But that was easier said than done when you were on the receiving end. Her heart went out to both Ms. Dalton and Enid. She knew only too well what it was like having conversations end abruptly when you walked into a room, having people look at you as if you'd just sprouted another head or something. People had treated her like that when Jessica had been picked up at an off-limits bar during a wild brawl—and had let the police believe she was Elizabeth. The next day everyone at school was smirking behind her back. Elizabeth would never forget what a miserable time that had been.

She went back to the "Eyes and Ears" column she was working on. News about the upcoming dance. A story about Winston Egbert and his wrong turn down a one-way street during drivers' ed. Thinking of Winston, her mind flashed to the last line from George's letter:

P.P.S. Say hi to my buddy Winston.

Was Winston really such a good buddy? Elizabeth was determined to find out.

"Sure, Liz, I knew George had been writing to Enid." Winston sat hunched on the bleachers, watching basketball practice. "But I never thought it was any big deal. You know, like he and Enid were—were—uh—"

"I get the message, Win. You knew that Enid and George were just friends, right? That Enid was only trying to help George?"

"Yeah, that's it." He relaxed. Underneath all his clowning, Winston was really very shy.

She took a deep breath. "Win, did you by any chance tell Ronnie Edwards about the letters?"

Winston shot her a startled look, "Why would I do a thing like that? I hardly even know Ronnie.

What's he got to do with it, anyway?" He turned his attention back to the court. "Hey, check out that drive shot. Way to go, Wilkins!" he bellowed down to Todd, who flashed him a grin and blew Elizabeth a kiss. Even with his shirt stuck to his chest in sweaty patches, Todd looked beautiful to Elizabeth.

"The thing is," she pressed on, "*someone* told Ronnie about the letters, and Enid thinks it was me."

"Gosh, Liz, that's awful!"

She sighed. "Tell me about it."

"What're you going to do?"

"What I'm trying to do is find out who's responsible."

"You don't really think it was me, do you?"

"I didn't think you'd do it to be mean, Win. I just thought maybe you'd let it slip out by accident or something."

"Nope. I promised George I wouldn't. He figured Enid wouldn't want anyone to know. I mean, she's so straight now and everything. Anyway, George is a good guy. He's really changed. I can't wait to see him when he gets back."

"It sounds like he really cares about Enid."

"Sure he does. What're friends for? Anyhow, in my book a friend isn't someone who blabs a secret all over the place. I know everyone thinks I have a big mouth, but I know how to keep it shut when it counts."

Elizabeth looked at Winston with new respect. She realized she was seeing a side of him that few people were lucky enough to glimpse. It was too bad Jessica didn't see him as the sensitive, honorable person he was, instead of just a nerd who had a crush on her. In Elizabeth's opinion Winston was far superior to that stuck-up Bruce Patman, who roared around in that flashy car of his and acted generally obnoxious.

"I believe you, Win," she said, leaning over to plant a kiss on his cheek.

"Hey, watch it, Egbert!" Todd yelled good-naturedly from his position under the basket. "That's my girl!"

Elizabeth couldn't help thinking that if Winston got any redder, they'd have to paint a white line in front of him and use him as a stop sign.

Ten

Todd reached across the table at the Dairi Burger to lace his fingers through Elizabeth's.

"Hey," he said, "you don't look too happy for someone who's going to the dance tonight with the most fantastic guy on the West Coast."

She forced a weak smile. "Burt Reynolds is taking me to the dance?"

Todd laughed. "That's what I like about you, Liz. Even when you're down, you can always smile."

"That's me, all right—smiling on the outside, crying on the inside." Her smile wilted even as she spoke. "Oh, Todd, what am I going to do? I've tried everything, and Enid still won't speak to me."

The day before, she'd gone over to Enid's

house after school, hoping to catch her alone so that Enid wouldn't be able to run away from her. But she hadn't even gotten past the front door. Enid's mother explained that Enid wasn't feeling well and didn't want any visitors. Visitors! Since when had she been just a visitor? She had turned away in tears, so blinded by her hurt that she nearly collided with Enid's little brother as he came barreling up the front drive on his bicycle.

"You've done what you could," said Todd. "If she doesn't want to believe you're innocent, there's not much you can do."

"Something's wrong, Todd. This just isn't like Enid. She's never stayed mad at me for this long before. If I didn't know better, I'd swear someone was feeding her lies about me. But who would want to do a terrible thing like that?"

Todd shrugged as he stuffed a french fry into his mouth. "Anyone who's really your friend wouldn't believe a bunch of lies—not for long, anyway. If Enid really cares about you, she'll come around."

Elizabeth sighed. "I just hope you're right, Todd. Jess says I'm better off without her, but I really miss her."

"I wouldn't exactly call your sister the world's foremost expert on friendship," said Todd. "Look at what she almost did to us."

He was referring to the way in which Jessica

had manipulated him into thinking Elizabeth didn't care for him, and vice versa. Among other things, Jessica had led him to believe her sister was too busy dating other boys to bother with him. She'd told Elizabeth a story about Todd attacking her, when all he'd done was reluctantly kiss her on the cheek. Todd trusted Jessica about as far as he could throw her.

Elizabeth defended her twin. "Jessica means well. It really is nice of her to want to help Enid."

"I'm not so sure," Todd warned. "Anyway, you should go by your own instincts about Enid, not listen to Jessica."

"I'm not sure I can trust them anymore. This whole thing has gotten me so mixed up I can hardly see straight."

"As long as you can see your way straight to going to the dance with me tonight, you're in good shape. Just forget about all this for one night and have a good time, OK?"

"I wish it were that easy. I wish I didn't feel so guilty about having a good time when I know Enid will be sitting home feeling miserable. I mean, I know it's not my fault or anything, but I feel bad anyway."

"I know what you mean," he said. "It's like the time when I was a little kid and my brother got sick on Halloween, and he had to stay in bed while I went trick-or-treating. Somehow it just wasn't the same. Part of me felt like I should have stayed home, too." He grinned. "It worked out for him, though, because I ended up giving him most of my candy."

"I'm glad you understand, Todd." She squeezed his hand. "I hope I don't act too depressed tonight."

"Goes to show how well you know my tastes," he said, brown eyes flashing. "I happen to love depressed blondes."

"Thanks a lot!"

Elizabeth blew a straw wrapper at him, starting a war that quickly escalated and ended up with Todd the victor—thirteen wrappers to her eight.

Out in the parking lot he slid his arms around her, dropping a kiss on her upturned mouth. He tasted salty-sweet, a combination of french fries and vanilla milkshake. Todd's kisses were one of the things Elizabeth loved best about him. They were like Todd himself—firm, but so gentle. . . .

She wished she could stay this way, wrapped in his arms forever.

"Mom says that if we don't get our rooms clean, we're not going to the dance!" Jessica attacked Elizabeth with the news as she walked in through the door. "Can you believe it? It's positively *medieval*. I feel like Cinderella!"

Elizabeth shrugged. "So what's the big deal?

We've got plenty of time before we have to start getting ready."

"Easy for you to say. Your room is already so disgustingly neat. It'll take me a hundred and thirty-seven years to clean up *mine*," she wailed. "It's so unfair. Who cares what my room looks like? Nobody ever goes in it except me."

"And that's hardly ever," said Elizabeth. "You spend most of your time in my room, making a mess of it, too. Honestly, Jess, a person is entitled to a little privacy, you know."

"Mmmm," Jessica murmured, shooting her sister an oddly sheepish look.

She'd been acting strangely secretive these past few days, Elizabeth thought, wondering what she was up to. With Jessica, you never knew.

While Jessica disappeared into the Hershey Bar, Elizabeth set about straightening the few items that were out of place in her room. Mostly that meant books and papers. She was always scribbling something or other, and consequently there were notebooks and typewritten pages strewn about the floor. As she stooped to pick up some paper, she caught sight of a piece of pale blue stationery barely visible under the bed.

One of George's letters!

She realized it must have been there all along and felt a sick, plummeting sensation in her stomach. Anyone could have come along and seen it.

No, not just *anyone*.

Only one person in this house besides their mother would have gone into her room.

Jessica.

Suddenly it was all horribly clear. She was certain her sister had read the letter and told Ronnie about it. That would explain the strange mood Jessica had been in for the last week. Elizabeth knew her twin well enough to have a pretty good idea why she'd told, too. Nothing or nobody was going to stand in the way of Jessica getting crowned queen. Including Enid.

Trembling with rage, she folded the letter and tucked it away in a drawer. She was so furious with Jessica at this moment that she could have strangled her.

Eleven

"Enid!" Surprise was stamped on Nora Dalton's pale features as she opened the door to her apartment to find Enid standing there. "What on earth are you doing here?"

"I—I hope you don't mind, Ms. Dalton," Enid said haltingly, "but I really had to talk to you, and since you haven't been at school . . ." She let her voice trail off as she took in the unfamiliar sight of Ms. Dalton wearing a bathrobe in the middle of the afternoon.

"Of course I don't mind. It's just . . ." She touched her straight black hair as if wondering if she'd remembered to comb it. "I wasn't expecting company. You'll have to forgive me if I look a mess. I haven't been very well these last couple of days."

"I, uh, heard you were sick. I'm really sorry if I'm bothering you."

Enid reddened, suddenly feeling terribly awkward. She'd been so wrapped up in her own problem, she hadn't given much consideration to the ordeal her teacher must have been suffering at the hands of Sweet Valley High's gossip hounds.

"You're not bothering me, Enid. Come in. I'm glad you came." Nora Dalton looked thinner and paler than the last time Enid had seen her. There were faint purplish smudges under her eyes.

They sat on the couch in the slanting late-afternoon sunlight while Enid poured out her story. Talking to her mother had been difficult ever since the divorce—Mom had enough problems of her own without being dumped on by her kids, Enid figured. But she'd always felt free to confide in Ms. Dalton, sort of like an older sister. The three days she had been absent seemed like the longest days of Enid's life.

"I'm probably the last person who should be advising you about this," Ms. Dalton said quietly when Enid had finished. "But I certainly know how you feel. It's not easy being convicted without a trial, is it?"

"The worst part is knowing it was your best friend who put your head in the noose."

Ms. Dalton shook her head slowly. "I still can't believe Liz would do such a thing."

"Who else could it be?"

"I don't know, but there has to be another explanation. Why would Liz want to hurt you? She's your best friend."

"Maybe it's like Jessica said. It just slipped out. But she *knew* how important it was to me that no one find out. That's what really hurts. It's like my feelings didn't matter to her at all."

"What does Liz have to say about all this?" Ms. Dalton asked, her hazel eyes filled with sympathy.

"She denies it, of course."

"Have you considered the possibility that maybe she's telling the truth?"

Enid stared at the carpet. "I—I guess I've been too busy being mad to really listen to Liz."

"You should listen, you know. No one should be condemned before all the testimony is in. If you don't trust Liz, aren't you doing the same thing to her that Ronnie did to you?"

"I never thought about it that way," Enid said sheepishly.

"Talk to Liz. I'm sure she'll understand. She knows how upset you've been. Sometimes people don't think things through when they're hurting."

Enid got the feeling Ms. Dalton knew all too well what she was going through. The latest rumor around school was that Lila's father had broken off with her.

91

"I doubt if Liz is still speaking to me," Enid said. "I haven't exactly been overly friendly to her lately."

"I don't think it's ever too late to say you're sorry in a situation like this, Enid."

Impulsively Enid threw her arms around her teacher. "You know something? I suddenly feel about a hundred pounds lighter. Even if I don't have a date for the dance," she ended on a glum note.

"Why not go alone then?" Ms. Dalton suggested. "Just because you don't have a date, that's no reason to stay home. Plenty of kids go without dates. Just hold your head up, that's what counts. You might even surprise yourself and have a good time."

"Do you really think I should?"

"Of course I do! I'd go with you myself, if it weren't for—" She broke off, clearly uncomfortable about discussing her own problem with Enid.

"Oh, Ms. Dalton," Enid cried, "it's so unfair! I hate what everyone's been saying about you!"

"Enid," she said, her voice catching a little, "I probably shouldn't be telling you this, but I've been thinking quite seriously about resigning. I've spoken to Mr. Cooper about it, and he—"

"No!" Enid leaped to her feet in a blaze of indignation. "You can't. You can't just quit!

What about all that stuff you just told me? How can you expect me to hold my head up if you won't do the same?"

Ms. Dalton was staring at her with a dazed expression. "You don't understand, Enid. It's not the same thing."

"Why isn't it? We've both been accused of something we didn't do. What's the difference?"

All the tears Enid had been holding back now streamed down her cheeks. She got up and grabbed her jacket, suddenly feeling as if Ms. Dalton had abandoned her.

"Running away is running away—no matter what excuses you make!" Enid cried as she stumbled blindly toward the door.

She was gone before Ms. Dalton could reply.

The doorbell rang as Enid was applying a final coat of polish to her nails. She was so nervous that the noise startled her into knocking the bottle across her dressing table in a splash of pale pink.

"Darn!" she cried, dangerously close to tears once again. But this time she was determined not to give in to them. She'd spent the last hour applying her makeup, and she wasn't going to let anything spoil it.

Through gritted teeth, Enid addressed her reflection in the mirror: "You're going to have a good time at this dance if it kills you, Enid Rollins!"

"Enid!" Her mother stuck her head through the bedroom door. "Someone's here to see you."

"Who?"

Enid couldn't imagine who would be stopping by at this time. It was nearly eight. Elizabeth would be too busy getting ready for the dance herself. The only other person she could think of was . . .

"Ronnie!" She jumped to her feet, her heart taking off at a full gallop.

Mrs. Rollins shook her head, wearing a mysterious smile. "I'm afraid not, dear. But I don't think you'll be disappointed when you see who it is."

Enid flew downstairs, forgetting that she hadn't put on her shoes. She came to an abrupt halt when she reached the living room.

"George!" she gasped in disbelief.

This *couldn't* be the same George Warren she'd last seen two years ago. The boy standing before her now was at least a foot taller. A tower of tanned muscle topped by a gorgeous white smile and the sexiest eyes Enid had ever been hypnotized by. He was dressed in a suit and tie that made him look even more irresistible. She stepped forward as if in a trance to take the hand he held out to her.

"I know I should have called first," he said in a deep baritone, "but I was afraid maybe you'd tell me not to come over. Somehow I just couldn't stand the idea of not being able to see you, Enid."

"I—I'm glad you came, George," she stammered, finally regaining her senses. "Oh, George, I can't believe it's *you*. You've really changed!"

"So have you." He laughed. "For the better, too. I remember you when you were a skinny kid with bangs that kept falling in your eyes."

"And braces," Enid said. "Don't forget the braces."

"How could I?"

They both laughed. Within minutes, they were chatting away as if they'd seen each other only yesterday. Even more astounding than the physical transformation George had undergone, was the change in George's personality. Enid was utterly entranced. Gone was the angry, sullen boy who had blamed the world for his problems. George was now a responsible young man, a good student, and—he informed Enid to her delight—he had been accepted to Sweet Valley College for the next semester.

Of course, she'd known from his letters that he'd changed, but she'd escaped the full impact of it until just this moment. Besides, how could she have known from his letters how absolutely gorgeous he'd become? Enid couldn't stop looking at him.

"Listen, Enid," George said, engulfing her hand in his large, warm grasp, "I just talked to Winston, and he told me everything that's been going on. I just want you to know I'm really sorry if my letters got you into any trouble."

"Trouble?" Enid forgot she'd ever had any troubles. The electric sensation of his touch traveled up her arm, tingling throughout her body.

"About the letters, though," he went on, "I have to tell you they were all that kept me going in the beginning when things were really rough. I could see how much you'd changed, and it really inspired me. You believed in me when I couldn't believe in myself. I guess that's why I wanted to see you—so I could thank you in person."

"Thank me?" Enid knew she was starting to sound like a parrot, but whenever she looked into those clear gray eyes, anything brilliant she might have said simply fizzled away.

"Yeah, and to ask you something." He cleared his throat. "I know it's kind of the last minute and all, but Winston told me about your boyfriend breaking your date for the dance, and I was just wondering . . ."

Enid's voice returned all of a sudden, loud and clear. "Ronnie's not my boyfriend," she broke in. "As a matter of fact, I'm not sure he ever was. And, yes, George, I'd *love* to go to the dance with you."

96

He broke into a mile-wide grin. "When I saw you in that dress, I was sure I was too late. I figured some other lucky guy had beaten me to it."

"You look pretty special yourself," she noted, admiring his neatly pressed slacks and dark wool blazer. "Why so dressed up?"

"Well, you see it's like this. I was hoping you'd take one look and figure a clean-cut, preppy type like me was too good to go to waste."

He handed her a small white florist's box he'd been concealing behind his back. Inside was a dewy white orchid corsage tied with a purple bow.

"George—you liar!" Enid's eyes filled with tears in spite of the fact that she was grinning. "You knew all along I didn't have a date!"

"What's the difference? You do now. Isn't that all that matters?"

When they reached the front door, George looked down and started to laugh.

"What's so funny?" she demanded.

"Haven't you forgotten something?" he asked.

Enid glanced down at her feet. "My shoes!"

"Never mind, I like you barefoot."

George wrapped his arms around her, drawing her into a gentle, tentative kiss. His lips were warm and sweet, sending waves of pleasure rippling up her backbone. She curled her hand around the back of his neck, holding him closer as their kiss deepened.

At that moment Enid would have walked barefoot over hot coals to go to the dance with George.

Twelve

"Well—how do I look?"

Jessica twirled before her sister. She looked stunning in a slinky red silk formal with a wide embroidered belt and black sandal heels. Long rhinestone earrings dangled from her ears. She looked as though she'd stepped out of the pages of *Cosmopolitan*—which was exactly the look she was after.

"You look sexy, if that's what you want to know," commented Elizabeth, scarcely looking up from the ironing board as she finished pressing the ruffled hem of her own slightly less revealing voile gown. "Are you sure Ronnie can handle it?"

"You act like Ronnie's my boyfriend, for heaven's sake." Jessica sighed. "I *told* you, Liz, I'm only doing this as a favor to Enid."

"Yes, that's right—you did tell me something like that." Elizabeth pressed down hard on the ruffle, imagining it was Jessica's head she was flattening.

"Really, Liz, you've been acting very strange the past couple of hours," Jessica noted, narrowing her beautifully made-up turquoise eyes. "What's wrong with you, anyway?"

"Nothing, absolutely nothing. What could possibly be wrong?"

"Well, I don't know, but you've been looking at me like I was the Boston Strangler or something. It's giving me the creeps! Are you mad at me?"

"Mad? How could I be mad at *you*, Jess?" Elizabeth asked sweetly. "Maybe you just have a guilty conscience."

Jessica frowned, tapping her enameled nails against the dresser. "What would I have to feel guilty about? I haven't done anything wrong."

"In that case, you have nothing to worry about."

"Honestly, Lizzie, I don't know what gets into you sometimes. I should think you'd be eternally grateful to me for all the sacrifices I'm making!"

"Oh, I am, I am. I'm just trying to think of a way to show my appreciation for everything you've done."

"You are?" Jessica's expression brightened.

100

"Sure. I want to see you get everything you deserve."

"You're a doll, Liz. I take back all those mean things I said." She went back to admiring her reflection in the full-length mirror. "What do you think—should I put my hair up or leave it down?"

"Better leave it down. You might have trouble with the crown otherwise."

"Oh, Lizzie!" she shrieked. "Do you really think I'll get it?"

"Don't you always get what you want?"

"I certainly hope so tonight. I've been wanting to go out with Bruce Patman since we were freshmen. This is my big chance. Finally. Oh, I can hardly wait!"

"I wouldn't get too excited if I were you." Elizabeth unplugged the iron. "You know the old saying about counting your chickens before they're hatched."

"Tell it to Winston *Egg*-bert. Can you believe he's even running for king? Honestly, I don't know how he even got nominated in the first place."

"Oh, I don't know. I happen to think Winston would make some lucky girl a fantastic king."

Jessica wrinkled her nose. "Ugh! More like court jester." She sailed toward the door in a cloud of perfume. "Come on, Lizzie, will you please hurry up. Our dates will be here practically any second!"

It would be the first time in their lives that Jessica was on time and Elizabeth wasn't. Usually it was the other way around, with Jessica keeping everyone waiting . . . and waiting. To Jessica's way of thinking, nothing ever really started until she arrived anyway, so why hurry?

"I'm coming, I'm coming," Elizabeth muttered, a sly smile flickering across her innocent features. It was the first genuine smile she'd managed in the past week. She was about to teach her dear sister a lesson she wouldn't soon forget.

The school gym, transformed into a fairyland by tiny lights and shimmery decor, was packed by the time Elizabeth and Jessica arrived with Todd and Ronnie at eight-thirty. The dance floor was crowded with couples moving to the driving beat of the music under flashes of starry light cast by a huge mirrored ball on the ceiling. The Droids were in fine form, with Dana belting out a steamy Linda Ronstadt tune.

"I can't wait for the voting to start," Jessica whispered to Elizabeth.

"Me neither," Elizabeth answered, wondering if her sister would be so anxious to win if she knew what was in store for her.

Elizabeth spotted Caroline Pearce, looking hideously girlish in a ruffled pink organdy dress that clashed with her hair, and wandered casually over to whisper something in her ear. Caroline smiled, her eyes widening. The minute Elizabeth walked off, Caroline was busy gabbing to the person beside her.

Elizabeth figured it wouldn't take long for word to spread now that Caroline was in charge.

Elizabeth was dancing with Todd when a stir at the entrance nudged her out of her blissful trance. She craned her head to see what the commotion was all about and caught sight of Ms. Dalton sailing through the crowd with her head held high.

"I wondered if she was going to show," Elizabeth said. "I saw her name on the chaperon list, but I figured she'd still be too sick to come."

"Looks like she made a miraculous recovery," Todd observed appreciatively.

It was true that Ms. Dalton had never looked prettier. She wore a long velvet skirt and an old-fashioned blouse with lots of ruffles and tucks. Her hair was perfect, and she had a silk rose pinned over one ear. It was obvious she'd gone to a lot of trouble to appear at her very best.

"Hey, Ms. Dalton—where's Ken?" a rude voice hollered.

She halted. Elizabeth held her breath, not knowing what the teacher would do, but her only reaction after that momentary hesitation was to smile even more broadly. She continued on to the refreshment table, where she was greeted warmly by the other chaperons, Mr. Collins in particular.

He took her hand and whispered something in her ear. Ms. Dalton nodded, and the two of them drifted onto the dance floor as The Droids launched into a slow number.

Elizabeth sighed in happy relief. "Looks like she's going to make it after all."

"People are still going to talk," Todd remarked.

"They'll get tired of it after a while and move on to something else."

"Let's just hope it's not *us*." He laughed.

"Hardly. What would they have to talk about? We're too boring. All we ever do is hold hands and kiss."

"Doesn't sound too boring to me." Todd's arms tightened about her waist as he tickled her ear with his lips.

"By the way," Elizabeth wondered aloud, "where *is* Ken? I haven't seen him. He's not still sick, is he?"

"You mean you didn't hear?"

"There've been so many rumors, I can hardly keep them straight."

"Well, I talked to Ken myself. He was supposed to take Lila Fowler to the dance, but when he found out she was the one who started that rumor about Ms. Dalton, he dropped her."

"Lila started the rumor?"

"According to Cara she did, but then I wouldn't exactly call Cara Walker a reliable source."

"If it's true, I'd say Lila got what she deserved."

Just like someone else is about to get what she deserves, Elizabeth thought as she caught a glimpse of her sister flirting with Bruce Patman.

Elizabeth couldn't believe it when she turned and saw Enid floating in on the arm of an absolutely gorgeous boy. She was glowing with excitement, her cheeks flushed, her eyes shining. She wore a pale mauve off-the-shoulder dress that showed off her slender figure to perfection. Her hair was pulled back, anchored by delicate mother-of-pearl combs. The shimmering whiteness of the flower George had given her set off her radiant smile. Liz had never seen her look so beautiful.

She was dying to rush over and ask Enid what had happened and who she was with, but she fought the impulse. Suppose Enid snubbed her in front of everyone? All eyes were on Enid and her spectacular date as she sailed across the dance floor. Elizabeth couldn't risk the humiliation of having Enid cut her dead. Yet she would have given anything to talk to Enid, to have things the way they were before Jessica had ruined it all.

Todd had just gone off to the refreshment table to get some punch when Elizabeth noticed

Enid walking toward her. Her pulse quickened. Was Enid still angry with her? She felt the heat climbing in her cheeks as Enid approached. Enid wasn't smiling. She looked tense about something.

"Liz?" Enid placed a tentative hand on her arm. "Can we talk? I know you're probably furious with me, and you have every right to be, but—but I just want you to know how sorry I am for the way I've been acting."

"You're sorry?" Elizabeth was stunned.

"I never really believed you were responsible for Ronnie finding out about the letters. Not deep down in my heart. I guess I was just so angry at everything, I was using you for a dartboard. It was wrong. I know you would never do anything to hurt me, Liz."

Tears filled Elizabeth's eyes as she hugged her friend. "Oh, Enid, I'm so glad! I was so afraid we'd never be friends again!"

"We're joined at the ear, remember?" Enid laughed. She was referring to their marathon sessions over the phone. Her own eyes shone with tears as well. "I'm just so relieved *you're* not mad at *me*, Liz. I was positive you'd never want to speak to me again."

"How could I not speak to you when I'm dying to know who that fabulous guy you're with is? Enid, what's going *on*?"

Enid smiled, her face taking on a dreamy

expression. Quickly she filled Elizabeth in on everything that had happened.

"George is pretty special," she said, "and not just on the surface, either. I know I'd never have to pretend to be someone I'm not when I'm with him. You were so right, Liz—honesty really is the best way. I don't think it would have worked with Ronnie, even if someone hadn't told him about the letters."

"The fact remains that someone *did* tell," Elizabeth said. "And I happen to know who it was."

"Who?" Enid asked.

"I can't say, but I want you to know that the person responsible isn't going to get off without a few scratches of her own."

Enid shook her head in amazement at the way things had turned out. A week ago she would have wanted to strangle whoever had been responsible for ruining her relationship with Ronnie. Now she didn't really care. It was partly because of George and partly because her talk with Ms. Dalton had made her realize that a relationship that wasn't built on honesty and trust wasn't any kind of relationship at all. And that went for friendship, too. Friends had to trust each other, even when things got messy.

"You know something," Enid said, "I should really thank whoever did that to me. She really did me a favor in the end."

"Enid," Elizabeth admonished, "there is a point at which you can be *too* forgiving."

"No, I really mean it. If I hadn't broken up with Ronnie, I never would have realized how narrow-minded he was. And," she added with a sparkle in her eye, "I wouldn't be here with George, either."

Elizabeth hugged her best friend. "Oh, Enid, I'm so happy for you! I hope he knows what a terrific girl he's getting!"

"He'd *better*," Enid replied. "I'm through with apologizing for myself. Whatever mistakes I made in the past are over and done with. I learned from them, and that's all that counts."

"Hey, when you two are finished gabbing, I'd like a dance with Cinderella here," George interrupted, appearing before them with a cup of punch in hand. Without taking his eyes off Enid, he gave the cup to Elizabeth.

Enid laughed breathlessly as he drew her into his arms. "Liz, I'd like you to meet Prince Charming. He's got this thing about shoes, you see."

"Actually," George said, trying to keep a straight face, "I'm nuts about her handwriting. Even if she is a little strange, she writes terrific letters."

Enid pretended to be hurt. "Is that all I am to you? Just a pen pal?"

"What do you think?" George turned to

Elizabeth with a mischievous look. "Should I trade in my pen and paper for the real thing?"

"I give it my stamp of approval." She giggled.

As George and Enid whirled off onto the dance floor, Elizabeth noticed a number of people staring. Enid had certainly never looked so lovely. And George made her the envy of every girl in the room. Even Jessica had pried her eyes away from Bruce long enough to take a good long look. Ronnie was the only one who appeared unhappy; he was scowling at George and Enid as if he'd like to murder them both.

Enid might never make queen if he had anything to do with it, Elizabeth realized. Somehow, though, she didn't think it would break Enid's heart if she lost.

"They're voting now," Jessica rushed over to whisper in her ear. "Oh, Lizzie, I don't know if I can stand the suspense!"

Thirteen

A breathless hush fell over the gymnasium as the results of the voting were handed over to Ronnie, who stood poised onstage to announce the new queen.

"By a landslide," he boomed into the microphone, "the winner is . . ."

A few people were looking at Enid, obviously wondering if there was a chance she could have won.

"Jessica Wakefield!"

"I don't believe it!" Jessica shrieked, as if she hadn't known all along, in every inch of her bones, that she was going to win.

She glowed with a radiant sense of accomplishment. She'd worked so hard for this moment. Now it was all going to be hers! The crown, the boy she adored—everything!

She held her breath even so, as Ronnie leaned into the microphone to announce the king's name. It *had* to be Bruce, she told herself. Everyone knew he was the cutest guy in school. No one else came close. She glanced over to where he was standing, slouched against the wall, whispering into his date's ear as if he didn't care whether he won or not. How could any guy be so incredibly adorable?

Ronnie's voice crackled through the microphone as he read the results of the voting off a slip of paper. "OK, folks, are you ready for this? Can we have a drum roll, please?"

Emily Mayer, The Droids' drummer, obliged, as Jessica stood licking her dry lips. Each drumbeat echoed her hammering heart. *Oh, please, let it be Bruce!*

"Our new king is . . ."

Please, please . . .

"Winston Egbert! Congratulations, Win, wherever you are."

A loud whoop from somewhere in the thick of the crowd announced Winston's whereabouts.

Jessica listened in stunned disbelief. It wasn't possible! This wasn't happening to her. Her heart went into a sudden tailspin as the meaning of it sank in.

She would be stuck with Winston for the rest of the semester for any big school events.

Her vision of gliding across the dance floor in the arms of Bruce Patman vanished under a cloud of dark fury. Well, she wasn't going through with it! She would refuse the crown. Let someone else be stuck with Winston. This whole mess was the fault of Enid and her dumb letters. Let Enid be queen!

"Congratulations, Jess!" Cara screeched, swooping down on her with a fierce hug. "I knew you'd get it. I just *knew* it. Aren't you happy? Aren't you just positively ecstatic?"

"I'm so ecstatic, I could die." Jessica groaned. "Can you believe it? The big disco dance is coming up in exactly three weeks, and I'm stuck with Winston Egbert!" She was close to tears. "I was so sure Bruce would be king. Now he'll be taking someone else. How could anything so hideous have happened to *me*?"

Cara was confused. "But I thought you wanted to be with Winston. Everyone's been saying you'd really flipped over him. I thought it sounded kind of funny, since I know how crazy you were about Bruce, but let's face it, Jess, you *have* been known to change your mind on more than one occasion."

"I'd like to murder whoever started that rumor," Jessica muttered darkly.

Who could hate her enough to do such an awful thing to her?

Suddenly Jessica remembered about the funny way Elizabeth had been acting earlier that evening. She remembered Elizabeth saying that Winston would make some lucky girl a wonderful king. It had to be! Who else but her own twin would be jealous enough of her to want to stab her in the back? She'd always known Elizabeth was jealous. And why not? Jessica was a thousand times more popular, she told herself.

Jessica was glowering, close to tears, when Elizabeth tracked her down near the refreshment table. Elizabeth was smiling.

"Congratulations, sis," she offered. "You don't look too happy about it."

"How could you do such a horrendous thing to me?" Jessica hissed, her eyes throwing off sparks of green fire.

"I haven't the slightest idea what you're talking about," Elizabeth answered, smiling sweetly. "Would you like some punch, Jessica?"

"I'd like to punch *you* in the face! Don't play innocent with me. You know very well what I'm talking about. *You're* the one who started that rumor about Winston and me so that everyone would vote for him. Don't you dare deny it!"

"OK, I won't. I did start the rumor." Elizabeth glared back at her sister in defiance.

"How *could* you, Liz? You've practically ruined my life!"

"You mean the way you tried to ruin Enid's?"

Some of Jessica's anger fizzled. "I don't know what you mean."

"Oh, I think you know very well. You're the one who told Ronnie about those letters. You

113

purposely came between Enid and Ronnie just so you'd have a clear shot at being queen. Well, Jess, you got what you wanted. Aren't you satisfied?"

"I'm not going through with it!" Jessica stormed. "No one can make me. I won't be stuck with creepy Winston. I'll resign!"

"No you won't, Jess," Elizabeth said quietly.

"What do you mean? You can't tell me what to do!"

Jessica was so furious she thought she just might strangle her sister on the spot. Only the thought of spending the rest of her life in jail—away from Bruce—kept her from going through with it.

"You're going to walk up on that stage and accept that crown as if you were Miss America," Elizabeth was saying in a threatening voice. "Not only that, but you're going to love every minute of it. Or at least *pretend* to."

"Why should I?" Jessica demanded petulantly. She didn't like to admit it, but on the rare occasions that Elizabeth really lost her temper and told her off, it had the desired effect of making her back down.

"Because if you don't"—Elizabeth leaned close to make sure she didn't miss a word—"I'll tell everyone in school what you did to Enid."

Jessica was really frightened now. Deep down she knew what an awful thing it was she'd done. Not even Cara would have gone that far.

What would people say about her if they knew? What would Bruce think?

She gulped back the sob she could feel forming in her chest. Even if Elizabeth had won this round, Jessica wasn't about to let her sister think she cared. "Have it your way then!" she flung back. "But if you think I'm going to do anything really gross like kissing that nerd, you'd better think again!"

A devilish grin spread across Elizabeth's face. "Gee, Jess, I hadn't thought about it, but that's not a bad idea. You know, you can really be sweet when you want to. I'm sure that would make Win very happy."

"Oh, no . . ." Jessica began backing away.

Elizabeth advanced on her, step for step. "Oh, yes."

"Liz, you can't do this to me! Think of my reputation. I'll be absolutely ruined!"

"I don't think so, Jess. Who knows? Your reputation might even improve."

"Lizzie, please, have a heart! You can't do this to your very own sister!"

"Try me. Just remember, dear sister, who writes 'Eyes and Ears,' in case you're tempted to back out. I can put all this in the paper!"

Jessica sank down in the nearest chair in temporary defeat. Over the heads of the dancing couples, she caught sight of Winston, a huge grin plastered across his face, bobbing toward her.

She groaned, wishing the floor would swallow her up that very instant.

A roll from Emily Mayer's drum announced that the photographer had set up his equipment and the crowning of the king and queen was about to take place.

Jessica approached the stage as if she were about to be beheaded. It was so unfair! Why couldn't Enid have been the one to be stuck with Winston? Of course, she knew perfectly well why, but that didn't stop her from feeling a flood of resentment.

Meanwhile, she was smiling so hard the muscles in her cheeks ached. Under Elizabeth's watchful eye, she mounted the short flight of steps leading onto the stage. Winston approached from the opposite end, looking like a scarecrow in a tuxedo jacket that was a little too short. His knobby wrists stuck out as he reached to take her hand.

The crowd burst into uproarious applause. Jessica wanted to crawl into a hole in the ground. She'd never been so humiliated in her entire life.

"Congratulations, Jessica," Ronnie murmured as he positioned the rhinestone tiara on her head. "You deserve it. I'm really happy you won."

"I'll second the motion," Winston chortled, looping a bony arm about her shoulders.

Jessica winced, fighting back her tears. This was supposed to have been the happiest moment of her life. And it would have been if only Bruce were here at her side.

She looked out over the blurry sea of faces below. Only one seemed to stand out more clearly than the rest. Her gaze connected with Bruce's sly blue eyes, which seemed to sparkle with some secret message intended just for her, even while his arm rested about the shoulders of his date, a stunning, green-eyed redhead. If only . . .

Jessica was snapped back to reality by the blinding explosion of a flashbulb. She noticed that her sister was whispering something in the photographer's ear.

Suddenly he called, "How about a kiss for the camera, you two lovebirds?"

Jessica steeled herself for the inevitable, cringing inside as she was forced to endure Winston's damp kiss.

I'll get you for this, Liz, she raged inwardly.

Her last sight of Bruce from the stage, before he strolled off, linked to his date, was of a lazy arm raised in mock salute, as he called, "Way to go, Wakefield!"

Jessica longed to run after him, to throw herself at his feet—*anything*. But she knew she'd made enough of a fool of herself for one night. Besides, there was still hope. Despite her frustration, she wouldn't let go of the deep-down belief that someday, somehow, she would have Bruce Patman.

Of course, that would mean coming up with an entirely new plan, since this one had failed so miserably. But she'd think of something.

Didn't she always?

Smiling through her tears, Jessica allowed herself to be tugged onto the dance floor by an eager Winston, who was practically tripping all over himself in his exuberance. She closed her eyes, trying hard to imagine that he was Bruce . . . that she was floating in the strong arms of the boy she loved. But the image dissolved every time Winston's clumsy foot ground down on her toe.

Just then Bruce sailed past, nearly colliding with her as she stumbled backward in an attempt to escape Winston's murderous feet. He swept her with a long look that sent an electric shock tingling up her spine. There was a hint of invitation in his smile, and more than a spark of interest in his sexy blue eyes. Some of her misery faded. *Could it be?* . . .

Can Jessica play Bruce Patman's game and win? Find out in SWEET VALLEY HIGH #3, Playing with Fire.

☐	26741	**DOUBLE LOVE #1**	$2.75
☐	26621	**SECRETS #2**	$2.75
☐	26627	**PLAYING WITH FIRE #3**	$2.75
☐	26746	**POWER PLAY #4**	$2.75
☐	26742	**ALL NIGHT LONG #5**	$2.75
☐	26813	**DANGEROUS LOVE #6**	$2.75
☐	26622	**DEAR SISTER #7**	$2.75
☐	26744	**HEARTBREAKER #8**	$2.75
☐	26626	**RACING HEARTS #9**	$2.75
☐	26620	**WRONG KIND OF GIRL #10**	$2.75
☐	26824	**TOO GOOD TO BE TRUE #11**	$2.75
☐	26688	**WHEN LOVE DIES #12**	$2.75
☐	26619	**KIDNAPPED #13**	$2.75
☐	26764	**DECEPTIONS #14**	$2.75
☐	26765	**PROMISES #15**	$2.75
☐	26740	**RAGS TO RICHES #16**	$2.75
☐	26883	**LOVE LETTERS #17**	$2.75
☐	26687	**HEAD OVER HEELS #18**	$2.75
☐	26823	**SHOWDOWN #19**	$2.75
☐	26959	**CRASH LANDING! #20**	$2.75

Prices and availability subject to change without notice.

Buy them at your local bookstore or use this convenient coupon for ordering:

Bantam Books, Inc., Dept. SVH, 414 East Golf Road, Des Plaines, Ill. 60016

Please send me the books I have checked above. I am enclosing $_____
(please add $1.50 to cover postage and handling). Send check or money order
—no cash or C.O.D.s please.

Mr/Ms _____

Address _____

City/State _____ Zip _____

SVH—9/87

Please allow four to six weeks for delivery. This offer expires 3/88.

Bantam Books presents a Super

Surprise

Three Great Sweet Dreams Special Editions

Get to know characters who are just like you and your friends . . . share the fun and excitement, the heartache and love that make their lives special.

☐ 25884 MY SECRET LOVE Special Ed. #1
Janet Quin-Harkin $2.95

☐ 26168 A CHANGE OF HEART Special Ed. #2
Susan Blake $2.95

☐ 26292 SEARCHING FOR LOVE Special Ed. #3
Andrea Warren $2.95

☐ 26528 TAKING THE LEAD Special Ed. #4
Deborah Kent $2.95

☐ 26702 NEVER SAY GOOD-BYE Special Ed. #5 $2.95

You're going to love
ON OUR OWN®

Now starring in a brand-new SWEET DREAMS mini-series—Jill and Toni from *Ten Boy Summer* and *The Great Boy Chase*

Is there life after high school? Best friends Jill and Toni are about to find out—on their own.

Jill goes away to school and Toni stays home, but both soon learn that college isn't all fun and games. In their new adventures both must learn to handle new feelings about love and romance.

ON OUR OWN—The books that begin where SWEET DREAMS leaves off.

BANTAM SHOP·AT·HOME C·A·T·A·L·O·G

Special Offer
Buy a Bantam Book
for only 50¢.

Now you can order the exciting books you've been wanting to read straight from Bantam's latest listing of hundreds of titles. *And* this special offer gives you the opportunity to purchase a Bantam book for only 50¢. Here's how:

By ordering any five books at the regular price per order, you can also choose any other single book listed (up to $4.95 value) for only 50¢. Some restrictions do apply, so for further details send for Bantam's listing of titles today.

Just send us your name and address and we'll send you Bantam Book's SHOP AT HOME CATALOG!